The Warriors In The Bible

Sapphire Scarlett

DREAM TO Print Publishing™

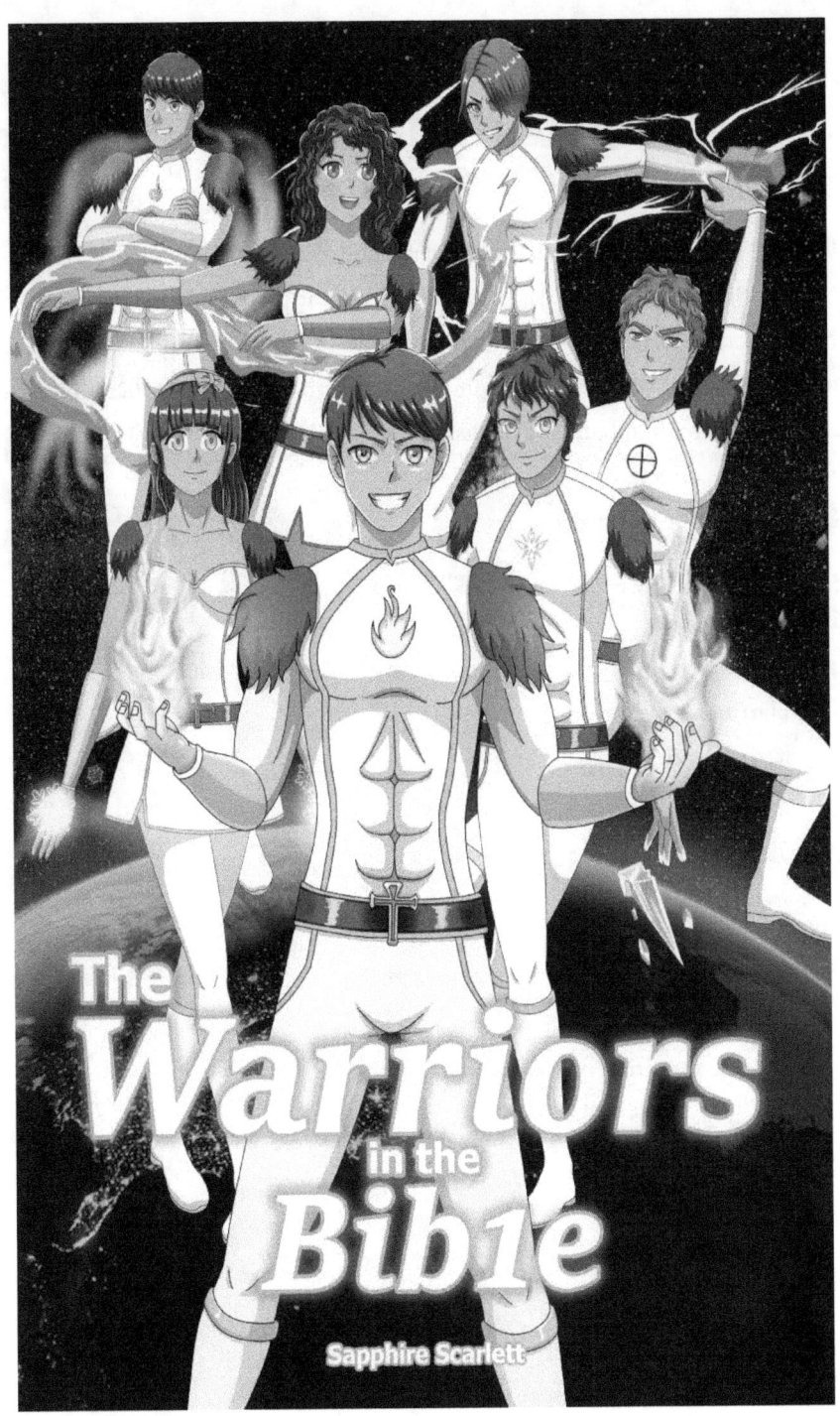

The Warriors in the Bible

Sapphire Scarlett

The Warriors In The Bible

This book is a work of fiction. The events and characters described herein are imaginary and are not intended to refer to specific places or living persons. The opinions expressed in this manuscript are solely the opinions of the author and do not represent the opinions or thoughts of the publisher. The author has represented and warranted full ownership and/or legal rights to publish all the materials in this book.

Acknowledgements

I dedicate this book to my mom Yanique Harris for all of her love and encouragement in helping me to publish this book.

Table of Contents

One

THE TRAIL OF THE BEGINNING OF THE WARRIORS!

Long ago, when heaven and earth were created by God, the rest of the planets were like the earth with its moon. Mercury and Venus looked like the earth with the sun, but everything changed when the moons began to crumble and turn the planets deadly. The people on the planets turned into stone. Mercury was also affected by the sunlight and the moons. Only the earth was not affected. The warriors appeared in the year 1414 but disappeared in the year 1996 after their long year fight with Satan and his demons. This was all in the bible. No one knows where the warriors are except God. The bible closed.

It was 2014 in a gray house; two girls were sleeping in each room.

It was 7:30 a.m. "Sapphire, Britannia, wake up. You're going to be late!" yelled their mother.

The two girls moan. "Huh? [GAPED] AAAHHH!!!!!" "Mom, why didn't you wake us up earlier??!," yelled Britannia. "No.

It's time; we are going to be late. Let's go." said Sapphire.

They ran down the stairs. "Here, you guys go. Cinnamon bread with butter." "Thanks, mom." We're off!" "See you later. Oh, I almost forgot."

"Huh? What is it?"

Mom - "Your cousins and aunty are coming up from Jamaica tomorrow, Lisa and her daughters, Ally, Elizabeth, and Monica, and so are the rest, even your friends."

"For real?!," asked Sapphire.

"Yes, indeed," said mom. "I've already told your older sister, Sashell, and she's coming tomorrow as well. Well time is wasting you better go it's 7:38 a.m."

"Oh, shoot, okay, see you later!" said Britannia. "[CHUCKLED]" They both ran then turn sideways. "Bye, Sapphire!" "Bye, Britannia!" Sapphire ran and saw her, two friends, Amber and Rosie up ahead. "[GAPED] AMBER, ROSIE!!!!" "Huh?" They both turned around and saw their friend Sapphire coming up running.

"Oh, Sapphire!" said Amber.

"Hey, you guys?"

Oh, it looks like you're late too." "Yeah, you've woken up late, but in no time, we've got to go," said Rosie. They started to walk, and finally arrived at school, but the school bell had already rung.

"Aw, man, we're late!" said Rosie.

"Let's just go to class already; we're just an extra minute late." Said Sapphire.

"Yeah, she's right. We can still make it," said Amber.

"Alright, let's go."

"Welcome back, 9th graders. Today in history class, we have a new subject now. Today it's Friday, September 2, 2014. Our new subject is about The Warriors in the Bible." Everyone starts to talk all at once in a whisper tone. "Everyone calm down." One of the students raised his hand. "Yes, you there."

"Mr. Tate, are you sure we're supposed to talk about religious stuff on school grounds? We're supposed to learn about that stuff in church."

"Nonsense! We can learn about it. I've even spoken to the principal about teaching it to you guys it."

Sapphire, Rosie, and Amber arrived.

"Well, well, well, well. Again? You're late," said Mr. Tate.

"Sorry, Mr. Tate," said Amber.

"We're just a minute late," said Sapphire.

"A minute late? Well, I supposed you're right. Well, it doesn't matter. As for your punishment, the three of you are going to get the history books from the library. Now go, and don't take too long," said Mr. Tate.

"All three?" asked Sapphire.

"Yes," said Mr. Tate." They went to the library. "Man sending us to the library for the history books, but not keeping it in your class, what kind of History teacher are you?" asked Rosie. "Hey, at least this is getting us time out of class." Said Amber.

"But he said not to be late." Said Sapphire.

"Well, he's a stupid teacher anyways," says Rosie.

"Calm down, Rosie," said Amber.

Rosie - "No way, I got to carry these heavy books all the way to the classroom." While Rosie was still talking, Sapphire picked up another book.

"Man, these are getting heavy." Then all of a sudden, she saw a glowing woman with white beautiful weathered wings. "Huh?" The angle waved. She waved back. "Oh my GOD!!!!! Rosie, Amber!!!! Come here, quick!!"

"What is it, Sapphire?" asked Amber. They came to her. "Look, an angel is out there! Look." She pointed out to the window.

"Um, Sapphire, what are you pointing at?" asked Rosie.

"Huh?" she looked, and there was no one there. "But it was here; I swear it was here."

"The angel, right?" asked Amber. "Yeah." "If it were an angel, it would've stayed until we saw it, and that's impossible angels can't come to earth. God makes them come with a huge light, and if they asked for permission to enter, God would always say "no," and there's no huge light." "I think you were just seeing things Sapphire, come let's go before we are even later getting to class." I don't want to be punished further because I will cuss that teacher out. Let's go."

"Yeah, let's go." They start to walk out, and Sapphire quickly stopped to look at the window then left.

Outside, the angel reappeared. "Oh, Sapphire.......," said the angel.

When they were all in class, Mr. Tate greeted them with, "Welcome back, now passed out the books and sit down."

"Alright," the three girls said and passed out the books.

Then Sapphire started having visions of her family and herself in the cloudy skies. "Huh?"

"Hey, Sapphire, can you give me the book, please?" said her classmate, a boy named John.

"Oh, sorry, John." She gives him the book, and she sat down at her desk.

"What was that? A vision?" she whispered. "Is something wrong, Sapphire?" asked her classmate, who sat behind her, a girl named Daphne.

"I'm okay, Daphne."

"Oh, okay."

Mr. Tate - "Alright then everyone please turn to your books to page 708, that's where we will learn about the Warriors of God.

Then Sapphire had another vision. She was fighting a demon and won. Sapphire looked at her hands. She thought in her mind "W-What is going on? Is it because of that angel I saw outside of the window while I was at the library?"

A student raised his hand. "Mr. Tate, can you move the curtains. It's bright outside today, and I can hardly see the book page numbers" "MH! You're right. Okay, I'll go move the curtains." He walked towards the curtains; then, Sapphire had another vision. It was the sun and her glowing with the same light, then she saw a man and a woman. In the background, there was a golden kingdom. The man reached out his hand to Sapphire, and she took his hand. Sapphire put her hand on her head and leaned on it, closing her. Then the teacher opens up the curtains, and the waves of sunlight hit the class. "There! Better?"

ALL: "Yeah!"

Sapphire quickly looked at the sunlight and saw a woman coming down with her hands out.

"Alright now begin the lesson," said Mr. Tate

"Why didn't you turn on the lights?" asked Amber.

"Oh my God, why didn't I think about that?" He closed the curtains; the women vanished.

".........no........," said Sapphire in a tiny voice.

He turns on the light. "Okay, ready, everybody?"

All: "Yes!"

The teacher starts to read, but then Sapphire had another vision of a female who looks exactly like her who's being pulled away. Sapphire was sweating and screaming. "[SCREAMED]!!!!!!" she fainted.

"Oh my God!!" yelled the students.

"What happened to Sapphire?" The teacher went to her and felt her pulse. "Everyone calmed down. She's still alive. She just fainted; would someone please assist her to the nurse?"

"I will." said a boy name Tyron. He assisted Sapphire to the nurse's office.

Sapphire was having a nightmare. She was in heaven. All the planets were turning into deadly atmospheres. She saw the same guy who was putting his hand out, sealing a ghost who also looks exactly like her. Then time skip, she was fighting the girl who looks exactly like her. Then she freed her, and they were reunited. But she went with Satan with tears on her eyes. "....no.... No....-" Sapphire woke up. "NO!!!" She reached her hand out, and she was in the nurse's office on the bed. "Huh?"

The nurse came in. "Hello, Sapphire, are you feeling okay?" "Oh, Mrs. Vanilla.
I'm sorry, and yeah, I'm okay," said Sapphire feeling a little guilty.

Nurse - "Huh? Why did you apologize?"

"Because I screamed."

Nurse - "OH, well...apology excepted. You were sweating, so I'll get you some dry uniform for you. Here you go." She gave it to Sapphire. "Thank you." She left, and Sapphire looked at the dry uniform. She looked at herself, and she was all wet. "Ugh!" She started to change. Five minutes passed, and Sapphire came out of the room. "I'm all done, Mrs. Vanilla."

"Good, I've already called your mother, and she was really upset and worried, but I told her you were going to be fine, and she was happy. Well, you should go back to class, it's 1:30 p.m., and you got two more hours and 30 minutes left. I know you missed lunch, but I was saving this cup soup for you. Do you want it? Or this sandwich."

"The cup of soup," she answered.

The nurse heated it up and gave it to Sapphire. She starts eating it. Outside up ahead of the school, the angel who Sapphire saw appeared. "Oh, poor Sapphire...." "Well, Well, Well, if it isn't my other triplet sister, the Holy Spirit, Ida."

She turned around. "Oh, Narda. The son. How are you? It's good to see. Actually, what brings you here? I haven't seen you since the year 1997."

Narda - "Well.... It's complicated. Well, Jesus sent me here to look over the warriors, but suddenly I been spotted by Sapphire."

"And I also heard of that too." They turned around and saw Serita.

"Serita!" They both said. "Well, well, now the father is here." "[CHUCKLED]. Ida, you think it's time, huh?"

Ida - "Don't look at me, ask Jesus he's the one who sent me here." "Man, it been lots of years since we both see you, Ida. I felt your presence and aura; I just had to come to see my other triplet sister who I haven't seen for like 24 years."

"Well, well, if it isn't Serita, Narda, and Ida." Said an angel with another with him coming down.

"Oh, Ivan," said Narda.

Serita turned around with an angry face. "Hmph!" "Come on, Serita; you can't be mad for me forever. Just be glad that I'm here. I'm sorry that I left you for six years, but I'm here right now, aren't I. Serita? I'm very sorry." Serita turned around. "Oh, come here, you." She hugged him. Then someone closed Ida's eyes. "Hmmm......let me guess.... well it's obviously Moses." He let his hands out. She turned around, and it was.

"Hey, mosses?" said an angel named David.

"Hello, Ida." "Will you two just go out already?" Asked Narda.

"Narda, no way. We're just friends. Besides, he was born on earth, and I was born up in heaven."

"But remember, Kaguya was also human, and she went out with Jesus and made children with him," said Serita.

"And Moses was accepted by God to lead the people out of Egypt with powers," said Ivan. "And remember with Jesus. How he got followers, and Kaguya was one of his followers and even died with him, and they both fall in love. That can happen to you," said David. "But remember Jesus was reborn so he can come to earth. If he didn't come down here, he wouldn't have met Kaguya," said Ida.

"But you two have so many moments." Said Serita.

"Well, well, it looks like the three religions of the nation and Christ of angels came."

"Wait, that voice, could it be....," said Narda. Jesus arrived with light. All: "Jesus!!" They bowed. "He-He. So, I see you actually came Ida, but you got caught by Sapphire."

"Yes, Jesus, I'm so sorry."

"It's okay; Sapphire is a warrior too; she can see you also can the other warriors. I see that you also checked up on the others, too, and they got visions?"

"Yes, I think the time has come." "Yup, to fight, now that Satan knows how to unlock the seal because he has my angel fire in prison."

"Jesus, she wants to stay because she believes that Sapphire and the warriors will save her. So, does your father, your sisters-in-law, mother-in-law, father-in-law, mother, stepfather, even your own wife believe that as well? Remember, she did break her out when Satan possessed her. On the year 1996, on the battlefield before she was reborn." said Serita.

"Yeah, Jesus, she's right," said David.

"Yeah, she is. I'm worrying too much, plus my yellow aura is keeping her safe down there in that cell. Now that the time has come and Satan finds a way to unlock the seal, I got a plan."

Three hours have passed School was over. Sapphire put her hand on her head, walking home; her friend Amber came up to her. "Hey, Sapphire, you want me to walk you home?"

"Um, well I live three blocks away, now we're on the 2nd block, But okay." They walked and finally reached. "Thanks for walking me back."

"Hey, what are friends for? See you Monday."

"See ya!" Sapphire walked inside, and her mother was cooking some steak. "Hey, mom."

"Hey, Sapphire, I heard what happen. You know you're not the only one. I also heard it from Britannia. She also fainted as well."
"Oh." "Yeah, you want some yogurt?"

"Sure." She had some. "Hey mom, why are you making steak? Because your cousins are coming over who is already here."

"Awesome. Wait, they're sleeping over?"

"Yes, indeed."

"Okay, I'm going to put on my pajamas."

"Alright."

Britannia came.

"Mom?" "Don't worry, I've already heard; your nurse called me. It also happened with Sapphire, before you ask why I'm cooking steak with mash potatoes is because your cousins who are already up here are coming over and they're going to sleep over, plus Sashell is coming as well."

"WHOO-HOO!! I'm going to go put on my pajamas." 2-hours passed; everyone arrives in front. The doorbell rang. Sapphire opened it. "Hey y'all," said Sapphire.

"Hey, Sapphire," says her older cousin Tristan. "My mother cooked steak for us, and did you heard that our cousins from Jamaica and close friends are coming over?"

"We know your mother told us," said her younger cousin Allyson.

"Well, come in." They all walked inside. They all were in their pajamas and sat at the dinner table. Yanique shared the food. "Okay, you guys, after you're done, go straight to the hallway downstairs where you're going to sleep."

"What? Why not in Sapphire or Britannia room aunty? "asked Abigail.

"Because their room is too small. Besides, when you guys first came here, you always slept in the hallway every time you slept over, plus the apartment downstairs is going to be Lisa's house, so yeah."

All: "Okay." They were done finishing their food and went downstairs.

"Wow, the hallway still hasn't changed," said Meisha.

"True, hey let's go to sleep, I'm tired." They all blew up a bed and got on them.

"Hey guys, can I ask you a question?" asked Rihanna.

"What is it?" asked Sashell.

"Did.... Did you guys get visions."

ALL:" YES!!!" "I wonder where they were coming from?" asks Roderick.

"I didn't even tell my mother said, Usher. "I wish somebody would tell us. Give us an answer." Then a bright light appeared, and an angel was in the middle of them.

"[GAPED]. You," said Sapphire. "Hello, everyone. I'm Ida. The holy spirit angel."

Two

THE FIRST BATTLE/FLIGHT

O h my.........," said Usher.

"I-Ida?!" yelled Junior. "SSHH. Not so loud." She put her hand on her lips.

"It's you. It's really you. I knew it I wasn't seeing things. It's really you. I saw you beyond the library window. Why did you disappear when I tried to show you to my friends?" asked Sapphire.

"Because Sapphire, I just can't just show myself to normal girls."

"Normal? What do you mean by normal?"

"I'm saying that you guys are the warriors. The warriors in the bible."

"What??!" yelled Shquana.

"That can't be!" yelled Meisha.

"No way!" yelled Trishawna.

"Everyone, stop screaming."

"We're sorry, but we can't believe it. How are we the worriers?" asked Sashell.

"Sashell remember, the warriors did disappear 24 years ago. So, maybe we could really be them," answered Britannia.

"But you said 24 years, that was the year 1996. That will be impossible. Sorry Ida, I don't think we're the warriors." "Sashell, please, you guys are the warriors. Let me ask you something, did you guys had......Visions?" ALL: "…. Yes! ….." "Hm…. He's right. The time is right." "Huh? Who's right." Asked Gabriella." "You guys are going to be shocked. Well, I got to tell you. It's Jesus."

All: "JESUS???!!!" "SSHH, Keep it down. I have to ask this, did you learn about the warriors in the bible."

ALL: "Well, not really."

"I see. Well, I tell you. On the year 1996, you guys were reborn. While you were all babies, Jesus sealed all of Satan portals open to earth. For 24 years, Satan was sealed with his demons. You guys started fighting Satan and his demons in the year 1414 to 1996. Now Satan has found a way to unlock the portals, and he's coming. Well, technically, only the demons can escape; Satan cannot. Not even his son's. Lucifer Jr. and Satan Jr. Satan's new goal is to capture the Lying Sin. That will not allow him to escape; only his sons and his sons are very powerful. That's why you guys must find the Lying Sin first before they do."

"What will happen?" asked E.J.

"Chaos will come. They'll be unstopped. The only thing stronger than that sin is.... Christ. But forget about Christ, right now, you need to find the Lying Sin."
"Wait, the Lying Sin is inside of a person?" asked Allyson.

"To be honest, yes."

"That means that the person is in trouble." Said Abigail.

"Yes, God put a seal around that person, and Satan doesn't know where it is. That's why he's sending all his demons to get it; he's relying on his son's. They can free him because of the blood relation. Are you guys ready?"

All: "Yes." "Alright."

Down under the earth in a red burning kingdom called "hell." "Finally, the seal is fucking broken. HAHAHAHAHAHA!!!!!!!! I FOUND A FUCKING WAY!!!!!!!!!!!," yelled Satan. He pushed his red button. "EVERYONE GATHER UP IN THE MAIN HALL NOW!!!!!!!!" Out in the main hall, every demon was gathering up in a single file line facing forward. A shadow girl in a cell was using her powers to cover herself with dark shadows. She was looking at them.

"Wait, Satan found a way to unlock the seal? But how?"

"You, of course."

"Huh? That voice, oh no!"

"Hmm.......... What's wrong? Unhappy to see your handsome new boyfriend?"

"Getaway, Satan Jr.! Besides, you're not handsome. You only appear handsome because you have cleared the sins that were once in your heart from my mouth to make yourself look like this."

"Well, thanks to you. Now the Lying Sin is definitely going to be found." "Remember the warriors are there." "Remember they've been reborn because of you, because you don't want them to come to hell and save you, risking your life to save them. Been in hell for over 700 years. I doubt that they're coming." "[SIGHN]." He put his hand on her cheek. "Bye-Bye, sweetheart." He disappeared.

"Oh, God." Everyone was facing Satan, even the people who were once human and ended up in hell. Single file. Satan was on top with his son's right next to him. Satan Jr. was on the left and Lucifer Jr. on the right. "Alright, everyone, the seal has now broken thanks to God's little angel, Fire."

Everyone was talking at once.

"EVERYONE SHUT THE FUCK UP!!!!!!!!!" They all stopped talking. "Satan Jr. Get Fire."

"I'm on my way!" He disappeared.

"You and you go with him." They both nodded. They disappeared. Fire was in her cell, sitting on her bed closing her eyes: the demons and Satan, Jr. Arrived and opened her cell.

"Huh?" "Come on; my father wants to greet you and introduce you to all of the people in hell."

"W-What?" Satan Jr. grabbed her arm. "Ah!" "Just be glad that you're out of the cell and able to explore hell. You have been in that cell for over 700 years."

Fire – Let me go!"

They've arrived. "Yeah, here she is. This girl helped me find a way to unlock the seal. The seal to go to earth, and guess what, for the new people who just arrived, this is-" Fire attacked Satan by using a moonbeam.

"AH! SON OF A BITCH!!!!! UGH!!!" Fire was angry and panting. "Put this bitch back to her cell. NOW!!!! Before I contacted God and beat the shit out of her right in front of him!" They grabbed Fire and put her back in her cell, throwing her in.

"AAHH!" She hit the wall.

"Don't you ever attack Lord Satan!" yelled a demon. They closed the cell and left.

"[PAINTING]!!!" Then a yellow aura was surrounding her and healing her. "AH.... that feels so good." In the hell meeting, Satan was recovering. "Okay now demons get out, I already choose a target, this person, a grown-up male who lives in Hartford. Next time you'll choose the targets. If I call their names out.

1.   Zack
2.   Elisa
3.   Aleg
4.   Lois
5.   Trish
6.   Peter
7.   Glenn
8.   Garry
9.   Lucy
10.   Anna

"There you go. Don't fail on me. I'm going to contact God and let him know the battle is on."

"Father, I think he knows," said Lucifer Jr.

"Well, I doubt that. I'm still contacting him anyways."

"[Sighed]" Satan Jr. and the two other demons arrived.

"Is that little bitch in her cage?"

"Yes, Father. Who are the demons, and how much?"

"Ten demons are going out." "10? I think you need to add more. Add five more like Chole, Max, Elizabeth, Jade, Pat, & Stewel." "MH, you're right. Satan yelled into the microphone. "Chole, Max, Stewel, Jade, and Elizabeth you're also going as well." The five nodded. "Alright, now go!" The 5-D disappeared. "Now, I'm going to my office and communicate with God. I'll tell him to prepare for battle."

"Wait, you're going to contact God. I'm pretty sure he already knows," said Satan Jr. "That's the same thing I said."

"Let me guess the warriors, huh?"

"The warriors been reborn 24 years ago. They've forgotten how to fight."

"Both of you be quiet; you don't run my life." He left.

Satan was in his office. He pulled out his magic screen and called God. God picked up. "Guess what? The battle is about to start."

"I know. Didn't somebody tried to tell you that?"

"Shit, but your warriors have been reborn, and they have forgotten how to fight. So that means that I will win, and you can't tell them, not even your angels, because you didn't want to do it." "Because I've always wanted to keep my word. When the time is right, I'll tell them the truth."

"Selfish, I knew it. Since you're God, why did you let your angel stay in hell? She's suffering, while her sister TWIN SISTER is on earth, and you believed that she would save her even though she is also reborn with the rest of the warriors, and now they don't stand a chance against them; after 24 FUCKING YEARS!! Your angel...YOUR FUCKING LITTLE ANGEL has been here for 7000 years, and you didn't do a single damn thing. You're a terrible man God. You and your whole fucking family." God's eyes were in flames. He was pissed, and some angels in the background saw."

"Oh man, God is getting pissed." Said an angel. "You're just angry." "Angry?" "Angry that your demons lost to my warriors every time since 1414, and angry that you been kicked out of heaven and lost to the war you don't know about Fire, and that was kind of funny when she attacks your ear by using moonbeam. You're the selfish one, you keep pushing your demons selfishly while I treat my warriors nicely, and now that we have found a way out of hell we are treating your demons-"

"Don't you dare says that word."

"Nice." Satan's eyes were in flames. "Ugh! Just wait till the battle."

"Okay, bye!" He hung up.

"Why does he have to be smarter than me?!"

"Because he created you." Said Lucifer Jr. coming in. "Oh, never mind him. I'm going to watch the battle right here."

"Well, see you later."

Upon earth, Ida was ready to give them their powers. "Okay, you guys. All of and each of you are the warriors of God, some Jesus, and three guardians. Guardians appear!

Guardian of air guardian of fire, guardian of water, guardian of earth, guardian of lightning, guardian of ice, and guardian of frost. Jesus warriors. Guardians of God's heaven. Guardian of Kaguya, Guardian of Venus, Guardian of Mercury, Guardian of the sun. Appear. The little guardians appeared. "Yes, Ida." I'll show you to your owners." She lifts her wand up, and it started to glow.

Junior God Warrior, power lazar eye's, Meisha God Warrior, power of hyper beam. Roderick God warrior, power of Electric bubble, Rihanna God Warrior, power of flower bomb, Shquana God Warrior, power of petal dance, and Trishawna God Warrior, power of water syrup. They've started to glow yellow each of them.

"Wow." Said Rihanna,

"What's happening?" asked Trishawna.

"I feel so much power," said Roderick. Their guardians went to them.

"Now, Jesus warriors." Said Ida. She put her staff in the air, and it started to glow.

"Tristan guardian of fire, Jesus warrior. Roman guardian of lightning, Jesus warrior. Usher Guardian of Air, Jesus Warrior. Abigail Guardian of Water, Jesus warrior. Sonny Guardian of

Earth, Jesus warrior. E.J. Guardian of Ice, Jesus Warrior. Gabriella Guardian of Frost, Jesus Warrior." Their guardian went to them. They begin to glow each color. Tristan had baby blue; Roman had white, Usher had orange, Abigail had dark blue, Sonny had brown, E.J had blue, Gabriella had gray. "Now and finally, the guardian. A.K.A Kaguya warriors." She lifted her wand in the air, and it began to glow.

"Sashell guardian of Venus, Sapphire guardian of The Sun, Britannia guardian of Mercury." They went to them. They've begun glowing. Sashell was dark yellow; Sapphire had orange and red, Britannia had brown and blue. "Wow." Said Sashell. "Cool." Said Sapphire.

"Awesome." Said Britannia.

"Now guys said, 'Warriors in the bible, DIAMOND!!!,'" yelled guardian of the sun.

ALL: "WARRIORS IN THE BIBLE, DIAMOND!!!!!" They've all transformed.

They've all landed. "Whoa," said Sapphire. "Coo," said Rihanna. "You like your new outfits?" asked Ida.

All: "Yes."

"I love Nikes," said Roman.

"I like the outfits," said Trishawna.

"I like THE SHOES MORE!!" yelled Junior.

"SSHH!! Not so loud, Junior." Said Meisha.

"Okay, enough talking about fashion, the demons are going to attack right about- " BOOM!

"Now..." "Wait, were are the guardians?" asked Shquana. "Right here," said her guardian appearing, but as a ghost.

"We're inside you." "Oh." "Now ready to fight?" "No!" yelled Rihanna. "Don't worry. The first day is always the hardest; you'll get used to it," said Ida.

"Yeah, we're the warriors, we can't give up, in the bible, the warriors always fight, and they never give up, and they always beat the demons." said Sashell.

"Yeah, but remember we've been reborn." "It doesn't matter; we're still strong. Come on, let's get out there." They teleported out in front of the house.

"Whoa, that was fast," said Tristan.

"Of course, we teleport," said Sonny. "Wait, won't cousin Yanique will notice that we're gone?" asked Meisha. "Don't worry. I set clones inside there. Next time you will do it. No time, time to fight."

All: "[GULP]" Ida disappeared, and the warriors flew to the area where the demons were.

"Alright, anyone scared?" asked Abigail.

All: "YES!" "I see them, but first we've got to hide." Said Britannia.

All: "Alright." They hid behind the trees and poked their heads out a little.

"Oh my God that what the demons look like?" asked Allyson.

"They look…. EW!" said Shquana. "Ugly?" asked Trishawna.

"Yeah." Relay back to Shquana. "We've got to be sneaky." Said Roman. "I'm a little scared," said Sonny. "Man up, sonny. We got to fight," said Roderick.

"We need to fight and beat them, probably God will give us a gift if we beat them," said Rihanna.

"Yeah, like that will work," said Allyson. Then all of a sudden, Tristan flew in and used fire-breather. The demon's dodged.

"What in the hell?" said Anna.

"Look, the warriors!?" yelled the demon, Lucy. "Let's get them!" yelled Lois. They've started to attack.

"Darn it, Usher!" yelled Sapphire.

"Looks like we have no choice since they know that we're here." Said Britannia.

"We can't just leave usher there alone.

He'll get hurt." said Tristan. "Okay, let's charge in," said Abigail. They've charged in.

"Looks like the rest are coming," said Garry.

"Who cares, we can still beat them," said Aleg.

"Enough talk. Let's get them already. CHARGE!!!!," shouted Elisa. They've charged towards them and collided. The demons start to attack first. The warriors dodged. "Huh? What is my power?" asked Sapphire. She starts to fly back and bumped into both Sashell and Britannia.

"Oh, God! Oh, it's you," said Sashell.

"I don't know what my power is," said Sapphire, me neither," said Britannia.

"Ditto." Rely Sashell. "How we're going to fight if we don't have any powers?" asked Britannia.

"I don't know?"

Then Sapphire starts to look at the moon orbit light. "Sashell.......... Britannia............ Look!" she pointed at the moon.

"Huh?" "What is it?" She starts to look at the stars, Britannia started to look only at the moon. Sapphire saw the same female who looks exactly her. The moon was on her forehead, and her hand was reaching out to Sapphire. Then in the background zombie hands were pulling her away. Sapphire begin to glow, and so did Sashell and Britannia. Sapphire shed a tear rolled down her cheeks.

"No........................" The girl was screaming. "SAPPHIRE!!!!!!!!!!!!!!!!!" ".... NOOOOOOOOOOOOOOOOOOO!!!!!!" Sapphire begin to glow; everyone stopped fighting.

"Huh?" asked Abigail.

Sashell and Britannia also were glowing the same amount of power. "Everyone starts to attack together. Please," said Britannia.

All: "Alright!!"

Junior: "Laser's eyes!!"
Shquana: "Petals shower."
Trishawna: "Water, syrup!"
Rodrick: "Electric water beam!"

Rihanna: "Flower bomb!"
Allyson: "Rainbow shoot line."
Meisha: "Hyper beam!"
Tristan: "Fire flame!"
Roman: "Lightning!!"
Usher: "Air wind!!!"
Abigail: "Bubbles!"
Sonny: "Rocks!"
E.J.: "Ice beam."
Gabriella: "Frost beam."

The beam was aiming at the demons. "Ha! Childs Play," they said as they dodged the beam. Britannia was in front of them, and a wand was in her hand. "Circle vibration force field!!" The demons were inside the line vibrate circle.

"What the hell?" said Garry. Sapphire used physic and control the beam, and it absorbs inside the circle.

"What are they planning?" asked Max. Sashell looked at the stars and controlled them. Stars line arrives, and it went into the beam, but attack been absorbed into the star lines turns into a star, and it hit the demons.

All: [SCREAMS!!!]" The attack disappeared, and they fell down, hitting the ground.

"Crap, we're now injured, we've got to retreat," said Chole. "Yeah, let's go, by the way, that man didn't even have the lying sin anyway," said. Trish. They've disappeared.

"They're gone now," said E.J. "The man over there," said Allyson. "Don't worry," said Sashell. Britannia and Sapphire waved their wands and blue, and yellow dust came out. The man's heart been healed and went inside of his body. The warriors disappeared. They've returned to their house.

"Wow, that was awesome," said Sonny.

"It was, but now, I'm tired," said Roman. Ida appeared.

"Had fun?"

All: "Yeah!" "Told you, you'll get used to it."

"Well, we're tired right now. We're all getting some beauty sleep."

"Well, see you tomorrow," she disappeared. They went back to normal, and their guardians disappeared.

"Okay, we've got to keep this a secret. Don't tell anyone. Not even our mothers, nor our cousins and our closes friends. Agreed?" asked Sashell.

All: "Agreed." "Well, good night." She went under her covers. Sapphire looked up at the ceiling. She thought to herself: 'Who was that girl? She looks exactly like me.'

Three

THE BEGINNING OF THE TRAIL OF THE MARRY WARRIORS

I n a dark place, Sapphire was walking around. "W-Where am I? What's going on?" She quickly turned around and saw the same girl who looks like her, but younger, with two more other girls who look exactly like her. "Huh?" Then a man came playing with them.

"What is this. That looks like Jesus." The three girls evolved into teenagers.

"Huh? Is that me?" Then the illusion vanishes. "Where did it go?" It returns, and she saw the same girl being dragged from the

27

hands. The girl shouted: "SAPPHIRE!! SAPPHIRE!!" "W-WHO ARE YOU?!?!?!"

"Sapphire!!" She disappeared. Sapphire frozen and turn around and saw a huge red horn ready to gulp her. She screamed and woken up, still screaming. She got up and saw her cousins still sleeping.

"Oh! It was just a dream." She looks at the clock, and it was 6:00 a.m. straight.

"Man, what a nightmare." She got up and went upstairs and to wash her face.

"[SIGHED]" She looked at the mirror and saw the same girl crying. "Sapphire........." She backed up and ran. She was downstairs and saw her other cousin Tristan waking up.

"Tristan." "Sapphire? Oh God, what's the matter with you?"

"I keep having visions." "Of what?"

"Of this girl who looks exactly like me calling my name, and I also have more vision," she was crying.

"Calm down, Sapphire. Relax. When Ida comes, we'll ask her. Right now, we should get some tea."

"Yeah, sure." Seven hours passed. Everyone was in the hallway.

"So, Sapphire is having so many visions lately and had a nightmare today? Tuh, no wonder why I heard screaming," said Allyson.

"She's right. I also heard screaming. Sapphire, what was your dream about?" asked Rihanna.

"I was in a dark place, looking for a wat out, then I saw three young little Me's and a man. I think it was Jesus. Then I saw the same girl screaming my name. Calling me seems like she wanted help. I did wake up screaming, but as soon I went to the bathroom, I saw the same girl crying calling my name. I ran then I saw Tristan. What is this, why do I have so many visions?"

"Sapphire relax, remember lots of people have visions too and remember before you found out we were the warriors we also had nightmares like crazy," said E.J.

"Yeah, you're probably right." Then Ida appeared. "Something wrong, Sapphire?"

"Yes! Indeed yes! I saw a girl who looked exactly like me." Ida's eyes were big and wide, and her heart was beating fast.

"Do you know who these females are, are they me or my sisters?" "Sisters?" asked Britannia.

"Sapphire, Britannia and I are your sisters," said Sashell. "So is Latanya, Davaiya, Shovon, and Shavaughn," said Britannia.

"Who are they?" asked Usher. "They're sisters from their father's side." Said Abigail.

"Oh!" "Ida, can you tell me who they are?" asked Sapphire. "Sapphire, I can't give you that answer."

"What? Why?!" "Because I just can't tell you. I'm so sorry."

"So, you know the answer, right?" "I do Sapphire, but God forbid me to answer that."

"Oh." Yanique was coming, Ida disappeared.

"Guys, guess what? What?" asked. Allyson, Roderick, Roman, Sonny, Junior, Shquana.

"Your cousins and friends from Jamaica are coming over today." All: "For real?"

"Yes, for real. I'm already cooking dinner; it's going to be a feast Today." She left.

"Wait, how did mom cook food that fast. I didn't smell the food." Said Britannia.

"We got to get ready, our cousins are coming over, with our mothers. So, we got to get ready," said Roderick. They've started to get ready. Thirty minutes passed, and the doorbell ringed. It was their cousins and friends.

"Hey, you guys, how's it been?" asked Sonny.

"We been good. I can't believe we're actually in America from Jamaica." Said their friend, who's named is Winston.

"What up, Winston?" said Roderick and usher giving him a high five. "What up?"

"Brandon!" yelled Trishawna running up to him. "Trishawna!" yelled Brandon. They both gave each other hugs.

"Where' mommy?" asked Trishawna. "Outside. Where' daddy?" "He's coming." Sapphire came outside and see if she will have that vision again.

"Come on. Where is it?" "Sapphire." "Th-That voice...." she turned around. It was her friend Julmarie.

"Hey, Sapphire?" "It's you. It's really, really, you." She started to cry. She ran to him and hugged him.

"[CHUCKLED] Man, you seem surprised to see me, Huh?"

"Yes, I am. It's been three years. I'm so happy. Well, we better go inside."

"Yeah." They went inside. Ida appeared above, looking at the kids who just arrived.

"Oh my......Why do I feel this strange sent?" The outer and dwarf planet little guardians appeared.

"Do you think it's them, Ida?" asked the guardian of Eris.

"I think so. They could be married warriors." Everyone was inside, "wow, whose house is this?" asked their friend Selena.

"Sapphire and Britannia house," said Allyson. "Your house is tiny."

"Shut up, Selena." Says her younger brother Cory.

"I'm just joking. Relax."

"So, where you guys are going to stay?" asked Rihanna.

"At the apartments, next door to your house," said Their cousin Serena.

"Really? Okay, good luck." Said Junior.

"What was that, Junior?"

"Nothing Selena, all I said was good luck."

"Man, you two like two argue a lot, do you?" asked their friend who's Winston, Julmarie, and Sheldon cousin Xavier.

"Not all the time."

"Let me ask you guys a question. Do you guys love each other?" asked Sashell, Sapphire, and Britannia little cousin Monica.

Both: "What? No!" "But, your blushing," said Monica's oldest sister, Ally.

"Can we not talk about this."

"You two will make a perfect couple," said Monica's older sister Elizabeth.

"Okay, guys enough teasing them," said Sashell. "Just saying." Said Monica.

"Well, everyone, since the adults are upstairs, we can go outside and play," said Roderick.

"Yeah, good idea," said Roman.

"We should." Said Gabriella.

"It's official. Let's go outside," said Winston.

Sapphire put her hand on her head, closing her eyes. She seems worried.

"Something wrong, Sapphire?" asked Julmarie.

"Oh, it's nothing, well, it is something. I think I need to rest in my room. I soon come outside." He grabbed her arm. "Sapphire, if you have something wrong, you can always tell me."

"Julmarie, there's nothing to tell, I'm a little sick. I need to go to my room as I told you I would come outside."

"Oh, Okay." He let go of her arm, and she went upstairs and into her room. She was on her bed.

"Oh, Julmarie, if only you can understand, I wish you were a warrior like I am. [SIGHED] Now, what were those visions I keep on having?" She looked at her mirror and tried to see the girl, but no sight.

"Oh man, wait, where's the female I saw this morning?" She touched the mirror, but no sight.

"Oh, I see. [Sighed]" Then all of a sudden she had a vision of a man with light carrying her.

"AH!! A-Another one! Was that Jesus? I'm pretty sure it was Jesus." Then she had a ton of visions now.

"AH!!" She was in a golden kingdom with flying angels. Right next to her, it was a woman with glowing light with beautiful feather wings, and on her left, it was the same men with the bright light. Right beside her were two girls who look like her, but one is a spirit who was floating. Then the room became dark. And formed into a cloudy Kingdom, but it was her cousins, sisters, brothers, closes friends, and herself. Then it was flying demons; they were battling. Then Sapphire was in a dark room and saw the same girl calling her name, reaching her hand out. "SAPPHIRE!!! SAPPHIRE!!!"

"[SCREAMS!!!!]" Roderick was coming up the stairs and heard Sapphire screaming. "Sapphire?" He ran up some more. Sapphire also saw Julmarie. "J-Julmarie?" His back was turned, and he was glowing red. Then a small planet that was red was in front of him.
"What the? Is that...... planet Eris?" Julmarie turned around, and his eyes were red. He said a low voice. "......... Sapphire..............."
Roderick was shaking Sapphire, and she was screaming.

"[SCREAMING]!!!!" Now she was crying.

"Sapphire, calm down!!" Yelled Roderick. In her visions. She saw the man right in front of her, he was glowing, and he went down on his knees and kissed her on the four head. Sapphire had a cross symbol on her 4-head, and she was glowing, and the sunlight hit her.

"[CRYING] & [SCREAMING]" "Sapphire!" yelled Roderick, Then Roderick had a vision that he was being carried by a glowing light. "What the?" He had another one that he was flying with the other angels, but they had a halo, and he didn't. He saw Junior, Trishawna, Shquana, Allyson, and his little sister Rihanna. They also didn't have haloes. They had a symbol on their 4-head. It was a crescent sign. He saw three Sapphire's. He begins to fell and had so many visions, he saw a bright light, and it talked, it transforms into a man, but his back was turned. He said.

"Roderick.......... Wake up." Roderick waked up and had something in his hand. It was dust. He quickly looked at the window and saw the same men, but his back was turned. He said: "Put it on, Sapphire." He disappeared. He sprinkles it on Sapphire, and she stops screaming. Roderick looked at his hand, and the dust bag disappeared.

"Wow, Sapphire, wake up are you okay. ANSWER ME!!! SAYS SOMETHING??!!"

"Something." She said, waking up smiling.

"Oh, thank God. Are you okay?"

"Yeah, but it looks like I attack somehow, by visions."

"You're not the only one." "Huh? What do you mean by that? Wait, you had visions too?"

"Yes, while you were screaming and crying, you had a symbol on your 4-heads. Then I had a vision. I was in heaven, but I wasn't really an angel, I didn't have a halo, I had a crescent sign: me and the rest of the God warriors, only the God warriors. I saw you with two other girls who look exactly like you, but one is like a spirit. I saw a man, a man with light; I didn't really see his face. His back was turned. He gave me dust to spread all over you, and you went back to normal. "I feel you; I saw Julmarie. He was glowing red, and with a planet right in front of him, it was red. I think it was a planet, Eris; I saw the same girl who looks like me calling my name; I think she tried to tell me something. I also saw a glowing man. He kisses me on the forehead."

"Well, Sapphire, you had a cross symbol." "A cross symbol?"

"Yes, I don't know how you got that. Yours is different from mine."

"Oh, I see, well we should go downstairs."

"Yeah, and next time when Ida comes, I'm going to get a good explanation for this."

"[CHUCKLED]" Down in hell, Satan was very angry at his demons.

"WHAT THE FUCK??? YOU LOST??!!!," yelled Satan in anger.

"We're so sorry, Lord Satan," said Chloe. "Sorry?! Sorry, won't win against the warriors."

"Well, at least the person we targeted didn't have the lying sin." Said Lois.

"Yeah, you're probably right about that, but I'm pretty sure God was doing that because he knows that the battle was going on."

"Well, Lord Satan, he's God. He's knows everything." Said Anna.

"Are you saying that God is smarter than me?!" He asked.

"What? No, my lord. I'm just saying." she said, scared.

"Oh, forget it, now you guys are going out again. I found a new target for you; it's this girl who works in a grocery store. She's at work right now, and the place is on Westland Street. Good luck."

All: "Yes, lord Satan!!" They all disappeared in red smoke.

"You do realize the warriors are going to be there to stop them, right father," asked Lucifer Jr. coming in.

"I doubt that all I care about the lying sin that's all, but I want those horrible warriors destroyed!! All of them killed."

"But not Sapphire, right."

"Well, not her. You just want her here."

"Well, duh? I need to be handsome like my twin brother, Satan Jr."

"Yes, and she my one-way ticket out of here, with Fire. Both of them together? That will be awesome."
"Indeed, it would. Now I'm leaving; I'm going to roast people alive now."

"Go ahead." The shadow girl was in her cell, sitting with the yellow aura surrounding her.

"Ah, that feels so good." Then it vanishes.

"Huh? Oh, no." Satan Jr. came.

"What up, Fire." "Go away, Satan Jr."

"Aw! Too bad to see me?"

"Yes, in God's name, yes!"

"Well, God isn't going to save you. It looks like he abandons you. What a selfish man he is."

"Shut up; Satan is the one who's selfish, and powerless against God. He always loses to him, and he used to treat you like crap before I came here. Now that I'm here he's starting to be nice to both you and your brother, Remember in all the previous years. Always lose."

"Yeah, while you're in here suffering."

"Hmph, you don't know anything about me, remember Jesus was suffering. I'm in his path."

"Yeah, but not in hell, and in a cell, for years."

"I may be suffering, but God is still protecting me."

"Where?" "I don't need to tell you where. You love to be noisy." "If I'm noisy, why did you tell me."

"Because you think God abandon me, which he did not, you just don't see it because you're the son of the king of all the demons, and you still had some ugliness in you, and you know that God is stronger than your ugly father, Satan. Remember, your father put my father in an illusion, but he came out. One day I will come out here." Satan Jr.'s eyes were full of flames.

"Alright, since I got a little ugly inside me, I probably need to wash them then." He went through the bars.

"Huh? Uh-oh." "Where's a God to protect you, where are the angels?"

"Leave me alone. Besides, they can't come to hell. You know hell and heaven need to be separate anyway, and I chose to stay here so I can be saved by the warriors."

"No need." He was close to her face. "[SCREAMING]" 5 minutes passed. "what took you so long?" asked Lucifer Jr. "Getting some things out of me." In the cell fire was placed on her bed injured, then yellow aura came and warmed her. ".... Fire......"

"Thank you." Upon earth, the gang was outside hanging out and playing. Sapphire and Roderick came out, and Sapphire felt a strange felt, her heart skip five beats.

"Ah!" she spits out blood. "Oh my God, Sapphire, are you okay?" asked Roderick holding her while she was on the ground. "Yeah, I'm okay. What was that all of a sudden, my heart seems it skips five heartbeats."

"For real?" asked Allyson coming over.

"Yeah! I'm going to the grocery store to buy meat. See you guys later," said Julmarie's mother.

"Okay, later, mom," said Julmarie waving. "Julmarie, you should come." "Uh, no, thanks." "Don't worry, Julmarie, I'll come with you," said Sapphire.

"Actually, we should all go. The grocery store is three blocks away from here," said Tristan.

"Yeah, good idea," said Shquana. "We should all go." Said Trishawna.

"Okay, you guys should all go; remember, all I need is a meat steak. Here's the money. Stay close together. See you."

ALL: "See ya." They started to walk, right now they were on the 2nd block by the store. Max and Lois were dress like humans.

"Alright, remember the plan, Lois?" asked Max.

"Yup." "Alright, Let's find the women and-" "Found her." "What, where?" "Over there, just standing over there."

"Oh, okay. Let's go over there." They went over.

"Excuse me, miss? We have trouble times, looking for the meat so we can provide for our family."

"Well, the meat is all the way at the back. Here I'll help you." They started walking to the back. "When are we going to strike now?" whispered Lois. "Soon. Not quite yet." They reached the end.

"Here you are, all of the meat you can get."

"Oh, thanks, by the way, can I ask you something?"

"Sure! Anything?" Max came close to her.

"Have you ever committed the sin that's terrible?"

"What...." Outside, the gang was walking. "Man, I can't believe that you agreed we hath to walk." Said Britannia.

"Come on; we got to do some exercise." Said Serena.

"Yeah, walk." Then all of a sudden Ally had a vision of a white planet.

"Ugh." She stopped and put her hand on her head.

"Something wrong, Ally?" asked Elizabeth.

"Oh, well, I just had a vision of a white planet above the sun; I think it was the planet, Pallas."

"What?!" Yelled the God, Jesus, guardians' warriors.

"It's nothing to it, just a little vision; we're wasting time. Let's just go to the store, look it's right there." As soon as they were getting closer, it was an explosion. BOOM!!

"Oh my God!" yelled Monica.

"It looks like it's over the Grocery store!" yelled Winston.

"We need to run back!" yelled Cory.

"Alright, but I need a closer look." Said Sashell.

"Are you insane, Sashell?!" asked Xavier.

"No, go back to the house; the rest of you who are up here, come with me." They ran out.

"Where are they going?" asked Brandon. "Sapphire," said Julmarie grabbing her arm, but he had a vision of a red planet.

"What the..." He let go, and Sapphire ran off. "Was that Eris?" Monica starts to follow.

"Monica, where are you going?" asked Elizabeth. "I'm going with them."

"Are you insane, you'll get killed."

"No, remember, Ally did have a vision. She saw the planet, Pallas. It said in the bible that marry warriors are from the dwarf planets."

"Monica, that was just a mistake."

"Mistake? Look, I'm going to see what's up with them, probably they can be the warriors, only the warriors can go through that mess. I'm going to go check it out."

She ran out. "Monica, come back here!" yelled, Ally. They all chased her, and she saw Sapphire and the others behind a tree.

"Huh? Look, you guys." "Hide," whispered Josh. They have been hidden, and they begin to Transform.

ALL: "WARRIORS IN THE BIBLE!!! DIAMOND!!!"

They flew out. "Oh my God," said Josh.

"They're the warriors?" asked Xavier. "Whoa. Monica was right. They are." said Serena.

"I told you," said Monica.

"What makes you think we're the marry warriors?" asked Elizabeth.

"Remember what I said. Ally had a vision."
"But what about the rest of us."

"I don't know, but let's see."

"No, okay, maybe Ally had a vision, but that doesn't mean she a warrior."

"Oh, you didn't see them over there, that's our cousins. Sashell, Sapphire, and Britannia. They've transformed. They're the warriors."

"But that doesn't mean we are. Remember, in the church; they said that warriors disappeared 24 years ago. We can't and weren't born in the year 1996."

"God's magic remembers. If it weren't for me, you wouldn't see them." "Because you were running." "Which means you were chasing me and didn't you say the warriors been reborn. Um hello. The warriors were right there."

"Can I make a confession?" asked Julmarie. "What is it?" "When I touched Sapphire's arm, I also had a vision. I was on planet Eris. I saw."

"See. Let's go a little bit near and see what's up," said Monica.

"Alright. Just for a little," They went to the grocery store and saw their cousins and friends fighting the demons.

"Whoa," said Josh. "Cool," said Sheldon.

"I see Sapphire," said Julmarie. "How can you tell, each of them is covered with golden light," said Sheldon.

"Take a closer look." They all did and saw.

"I see." Said Serena. "So do I.," said Ally.
"Hey, look, an injured person," said Winston.

"With her heart out," said Cory.

"I'm going to go help her."

"Wait, Sheldon, it's too dangerous," yelled Xavier. Sheldon picked up the women.

"EW!! Look at the heart."

"We shouldn't be here."

"Yeah, I know, and why do I see black spots on her heart?"

"How should I know." Then a demon notices them.

"HEY!! Look more humans. Maybe we should strike them." said a demon named Elisa. The warriors notice.

"What the...?" asked Shquana.

"Oh no," said Trishawna.

"I told them to go home," said Sashell.

"Oh, I see these warriors know these humans. Let's just destroyed them anyway," said Trish.

"Yeah," said the rest of the demons."

All: "No!!" The demons attack them; then, something saves all of them. It was both Sapphire and Britannia. They both fall.

"Sapphire!!! Britannia!!," yelled Sashell. Julmarie catches Sapphire, and Ally catches Britannia.

"Oh, my God! Sapphire, are you okay?" asked Julmarie frighten.

"How did you know it was me?" asked Sapphire, very injured.

"Because when I grabbed your arm, I had a vision of a red planet. Then I can see you under your bright golden light that's covering you."

"I see, you must be a warrior because I too had visions. I saw you glowing in a red aura around you with planet Eris in front of you. Julmarie."

"Britannia. Why would you do that?" asked Ally, crying.

"Because we're cousins. I have a feeling that when you said you had a vision of planet Pallas. I think you're a warrior.

"No...," said Julmarie. "Julmarie you were a great friend." She fainted. "No...," said Ally.

"Ally, I will always remember you." She also fainted.

ALL: "NNNNOOOOOOO!!!!!!!!!!!!!!!!!!!" They've begun glowing with different colors.

"What's going on?" yelled Junior. Symbols appeared on their foreheads. "I think their transforming," said Sonny. All of them were in a yellow bubble, and little yellow lines were coming towards them.

"Guardians of marrying warriors," said Abigail guardian.

"What? Are you saying?" asked Abigail.

"Sheldon guardian of Juno."

"Josh guardian of Pluto."

"Ally guardian of Pallas."

"Elizabeth guardian of Vesta."

"Monica guardian of Hygeia."

"Re-Re guardian of Varuna."

"Cory guardian of Ce-Ce."
"Selena guardian of Sedna."

"Serena guardian of Hamuea."

"Winston guardian of Make-Make."

"Brandon guardian of Ixion."

"Xavier guardian of Orcus."

"Julmarie guardian of Eris."

Everyone was just staring at them. "Oh my God," said Roderick.

"This can't be," said Rihanna. "They're the," said Gabriella.

"Marry warriors," said Sashell.

Four

NEWBORN WARRIORS

Y ou'll pay for what you did to Sapphire and Britannia!!"
Yelled Re-Re.

"Oh yeah, bring it on; besides, I don't think I will lose to a little girl like you." Said Chloe.

"Yeah, all girls are weak." Said Max. "EXCUSE ME???!!!" yelled all the girls, including the female demons."

"Whoops." "Next time, shut up." Said Garry.

Winston started to attack first. "Make Make beam.!!" It came out and some demons attack but the marry warriors spread out and they were beside each demon.

"What the?" said all the demons.

All: "Magic beam." It hit the demons, and they hit each other.

47

The rest of the warriors came in and used their powers as well. It also hit the demons.

"Damn it; we're outnumbered." Said Zack.

"We need to retreat." Said Lois.

"We got what we need for. Let's go." Said Max.

"Oh no, you don't! Take this.!" Yelled Serena blasting a beam at them. It hit them.

"Looks like we got no chance, but to fight." Said Aleg. Aleg starts to attack Selena. But Josh protected her by using a shield.

"Shit!!" He yelled in anger.

"Josh used super sprint, and he was confusing Aleg.

"What he?" "Don't worry, Aleg; I will help you!" Yelled Trish flying in. She used a dark pulse at josh, but josh stop running, the circled disappeared, and it hit Aleg.

"Oh, no." "That what you get." Said Sheldon behind her. "What the hell?" he used jiral ball at her back. Sashell also hit her while she was falling with bombs stars.

"Aw, yes." She said in excitement. Jade was three feet away from Sashell behind.

"I got you this time." She threw a dark ball at Sashell. She quickly turned around, she was about to protect herself, but too late she got hit.

"SASHELL!!" yelled Roderick.

"Don't let your guard down, kid." Said Chloe behind him. Roderick quickly flew away, turned around, and used an electric bubble at him, but he dodged.

"Oh, snap." Lois was behind Roderick and grabbed him.

"What the? Hey, get off me."

"Nice one Lois, now then hold him still...." He was powering up.

"SO, I CAN BLAST HIM" He shot a beam out of his hand. It hit both of them, but Lois was most likely more healed.

"Damn, should have given me a single."

"Well, too bad, at least we got him." Then they heard an explosion above them, and five warriors were falling down. It was Junior, Tristan, Rihanna, and Allyson.

"Man, five already?" asked Jade coming over. Then the rest fall down.

"Man, I guess it happens to you guys to, huh?" asked Trishawna.

"Yeah.... Aww! My leg and my whole body." Said Gabriella.

"We can heal you." Said their guardians.

"Good, but hurry." Said Abigail.

"Our hopes now are the Marry warriors," said Junior looking at them up above.

"And I hope both Sapphire and Britannia are feeling okay. I just hope that they're not dead," said Tristan looking at them. Up above the marry, warriors were flying around, and so were the demons.

"I'm all fired up for this," said Re-Re.

"Wait, where are the other warriors?" asked Cory.

"Look, down there." Said Josh pointing at them.

"They must be injured." Said Serena. "No time for talking, they'll join us soon, right now we got to take care of these demons." Said Monica.

"You think you can take us down?" asked Garry.

"We took down your friends. How are you going to stop us?" Asked Zack.

"Look, we all know that they took you guys on, more than us. I think it's our turn now," said Ally.

"HA! I doubt that." Said Peter. "Ready, you guys?" Asked Elizabeth.

All: "Yeah!" "Oh crap, they're going to combine."

Let's combine too." Said Glenn.

"Ixion power!" yelled Brandon,

"Juno power!" yelled Sheldon.

"Pallas power!" yelled Ally.

"Vesta power!" yelled Elizabeth.

"Hygeia power!" yelled Monica.

"Ce-Ce power!" Yelled Cory.

"Hamuea power!" Yelled Serena.

"Sedna power!" yelled Selena.

"Make Make power!" yelled Winston.

"Orcus power!" yelled Xavier.

"Varuna power!" yelled Re-Re.

"Eris power!" Yelled Julmarie. All:

"Dwarf planet attack!" A blue beam came out.

"Not in our watch!" Yelled Pat.

All: "Demon beam!" a red beam came out. It collides with the other beam. The two teams were at full power. Then both beams caused an explosion. Black smoke was covering them, and they were covering their breath. Then Lucy spotted both Sapphire and Britannia. Jada bomb right into her, and Lucy told her, and they flew down. Julmarie saw, and he flew down out of the smoke and headed towards them. Sashell was already healed and getting ready to fight but saw both Lucy and jade heading toward both Sapphire and Britannia.

"[GAPSPED] Oh no, you don't!" She threw two stars at them. Julmarie threw two lights dots at them, and they got hit.

"Yeah!" said Julmarie.

"Not so sure," said Sashell coming up.

"What do you mean by that?" he asked her.

"Look." She pointed. The smoke clears both of them are using protections.

"Aw, snap." "Yup, Their heading for both Sapphire and Britannia. We got to stop‑ Ah!" Sashell got hit by a demon. It was pat. Julmarie starts to get Sapphire and Britannia but stopped because a laser went in front of him. He turned and saw a demon coming down to him; it was max, then an electric blue water ball came and hit him. Roderick came over. "I'll deal with him, go rescue Sapphire and Britannia."

"Thanks, Roderick." He flew. Down in hell, Satan was watching the fight at his crystal ball on and in his office.

"Oh man, the demons are getting good. Hell fucking yes, but now I'm mad that the new warriors are here the marry warriors. I better contact God and talk to him about it." He pulls out he's big wide screen and starts to call God, He answered. "What do you want, Satan?" he asked.

"The battle is going great, just to let you know my demon's beat you and your son warriors and killed Kaguya warriors."

"They're not dead."

"What was that?"

"They're not dead."

"WHAT? HOW?!! I saw it with my own eyes."

"Man, you are so loud and can be angry most of the time. [SIGHED] Remember, each of my warriors is immortal even when their reborn, Sapphire, and Britannia are just knocked out. If they really died, both mercury and the sun will explode. Did it explode? Nope."

"Aw, shit."

"Remember Satan, the battle is still going on, and your demons didn't defeat the marry warriors. Hmm.... Well, I got to go, got stuff to do. I'll also be watching the fight as well too." He hung up.

"Oh, why does he hath to be smarter than me?"

"Maybe because he's God, and that's your creator." Said Lucifer Jr. coming in.

"I don't care, and that's not helping at all!!!!"

"[CHUCKLED], but I do agree that he's selfish for making he's own angel suffer in hell. "Damn straight for that."

"You mean, damn straight, you're right about that."

"Yeah, that. Where's your brother."

"Out there, tearing people."

"[SCREAMS]!!!! AAAHHH!!!!!!"

"Man, they really need to close that door. I can't stand the screams." Satan Jr. came in blood all over him.

"Wow, that was awesome. But I throw up a little bit, buy seeing an ugly old hag." He sat down on the chair.

"So, what's up? The demons are kicking ass?"

"Well, not quite. They did manage to defeat them, but not the new warriors."

"New warriors? Let me guess the Joseph warriors?"

"Nope, close. They marry warriors."

"Oh, the warriors who came from the dwarf planets in the solar system. Well back in the previous years, they're very good."

"True that. It was the year 1676."

"Yeah, and they were still good. But I just hope the demons beat them." In fire's cell, Fire was closing her eyes then woke up.

"I see, so the marry warriors joined, huh? Good for them. Oh God, thank you for understanding why I choose to stay here.

"[SIGHED]." "Then, yellow aura begins to glow on her.

"[CHUCKLED]." Up in above earth and the dark space, it was heaven. Jesus was on his golden chair in a worried face. "Something wrong, Jesus?" Asked Kaguya.

"Oh, well....... To be honest....... Yeah."

"It's about fire, right?" "Yes."

"Remember, she made this decision, and once you were suffering too back in the earth days. Fire is just following in your path." "I know, but I wish the solar system weren't like this." Kaguya put her hand on Jesus's shoulder.

"Jesus relaxes. The warriors will put it back the same way it was once, and we'll be reunited back with fire and Sapphire." Then all of a sudden, Kaguya felt a strange felt. Then a man came in with angel wings. "Kaguya."

"Oh, hello.......... King of Pop, Michael Jackson?"

"[CHUCKLED]" "What brings you here, Michael?" asked Jesus.

"God wants me to give this to Kaguya."

"It's about on earth with the fight with the warriors right now?"

"I don't know; he just gives you this." Kaguya went over and read the note, and she knew it was about Sapphire.

"I see. Something is wrong with Sapphire. No wonder why I had a strange felt. Thank you, Michael...Or should I say King of pop?"

"[CHUCKLED]." He left. "Well looks like I got to make another digital of me to show to Sapphire, and I got to communicate with the queen of mercury, so she could create a digital light to Britannia before they both get hurt very badly." "Yeah, but did you know something about Julmarie?"

"Of course, The prince/guardian of planet Eris. Sapphire did have a vision about him."

"Yeah, which I put in right after Fire put in visions inside Sapphire's head. Planet Eris does an orbit around the sun orbit directly. Julmarie can help you a little bit."

"I think he will right now." Down on earth on the battlefield, the warriors still continued their fight with the demons. "I got an idea." Said Jada.

"What is it?" asked Lucy.

"Let's hit the two girls down on the ground hardcore. Quickly."

"You're right." "Oh no, you don't!!!" Yelled Julmarie, He threw orange dots at them; they both dodged.

"What an annoying little pest." Red Lazor came, and it hit Lucy. "AH!" Junior came.

"I fight right beside you, okay?"

"Yeah, and thanks." Sapphire and Britannia had a dream. Britannia was on Mercury and saw people on them. She looked around. She was wearing a brown dress with a brown-black gem tiara. Then a wind came, and all the people there became into stone. She then was in a heavenly golden kingdom where she sees Kaguya. Sapphire had a vision that she was in a heavenly golden kingdom with two other girls who look like her. Then they both vanished. She saw a girl who looks like her with a man coming in with the ghost girl who looks like her. He put her inside her, and it was a spiral seal on her stomach. Then she felt a tap on her shoulder, and it was the same woman. She was glowing. She said, "Wake, up...." Then disappeared.

On Britannia's vision, she was back on mercury and saw the queen sealed herself inside Mercury. She felt a tap on her shoulder. She looks behind, and it was a woman. She was glowing with the sunlight.

She said: "Wake up." Then disappeared. Both girls were woken up. Sapphire was looking at Julmarie and saw a red light within him.

"W-What- That light...." Sapphire then imagined toward Julmarie about her vision a while ago. Julmarie turned around and said, "Sapphire."

Britannia looked at Sashell, fighting Zack then pat. She can sense an aura. A yellow aura. "This sent." She then had a vision of Sashell in a yellow dress. In the background, it was a yellow desert.

She said, "Britannia." Sapphire quickly had a vision of the same girl. "Sapphire." "I'm getting tired of this bull shit. I'm striking them head-on!!," yelled Jade. She put her attack on the ground.

"NOOO!!!" yelled Julmarie. Sapphire and Britannia got up a little bit.

They went on their knees. Sashell and the girl: "FIGHT!!" The attack hit them.

"NOOO!!!" yelled junior, but all of a sudden, there was a force field around them. Sapphire was orange, and Britannia was yellow. "What the?" said Jada.

Both: "DIE!!!!!!" A whole bunch of power and out of both of them and it hit the demon's hardcore. The warriors had a force field around them.

"Whoa." Said E.J. The demons suddenly disappeared. Sapphire and Britannia went back to normal, and they fainted. The warriors came to them. Then yellow dust came from the sky and healed the lady.

"Whoa. Did Britannia and Sapphire actually......do that?" asked

Five

THE LIGHT AURA

The warriors were just looking at both Sapphire and Britannia. They were very injured. Both Roman and Tristan went to them. Roman to Britannia, and Tristan to Sapphire.

"At least the demons are gone." Said Sheldon. "Nope, they're not." Said Sashell. "Huh?" But how, you didn't hear they said 'Die.'"

"If they really are dead, there would be blood everywhere, and I saw red clouds from them while they disappeared. They must've gone back to Hell."

"Oh, I see. My bad."

"No need to apologize. You're new here. And still, I can't believe you guys are actually the Marry warriors."

"We still can't believe it either, Sashell." Said Xavier.

"Well, the grocery store is destroyed.......... Huh?" Then all of a sudden, the store was back the way it was. "Who did it?"

"Probably when the yellow and blue dust from the sky came down, it must've fixed the store," said Ally.

"We'll let's go buy a steak. Our mother must be worried sick." Said Re-Re. Down in hell, Satan went towards the demons in their lounge.

"Uh-oh. Lord Satan is going to be very angry with us." Said Lois frighten.

"Lord Satan, we tried our best, but we did defeat the previous warriors and would've defeated the..." said Max.

"Marry warriors?" He cut off by saying it. "How did you?" "I saw the fight, you guys did a good job by defeating the previous warriors, but with them and the newborn warriors you'll be outnumbered now, But I see you still take them on. At least the target didn't have the lying sin; we'll you guys rest up; tomorrow is a new day. I'm going into my office."

In the Satan office, he was going to contact God, but his crystal ball appeared. "Huh? Another fight, but that's odd, all my demons are here. It showed the warriors, and both Britannia and Sapphire were glowing. "Oh, I got to see this, it looks like they're going to attack them." "I want to see that too, father." Said Lucifer Jr. coming in. "I'm going to play it on the screen so everybody can see it, including especially Fire."

"Good idea."

Upon earth, all of a sudden, both Sapphire and Britannia woke up in rage. Their eye's pupil was orange; they attack both

Tristan and Roman. "Ah!!" They both yelled. A huge yellow aura was surrounding Sapphire, and a huge orange Aura was surrounding Britannia.

"What is up with them?" asked Monica.

"I think they're possessed, but by what?" said Winston. "No, it's the visions with the aura." Said Sashell guardian.

"What do you mean by that?" asked Sashell.

"Sapphire keeps on having too much visions, it must have connected with her sun powers, and it created this."

"But what about Britannia?"

"Hers too, I know Britannia didn't have visions, unlike Sapphire, did, but Britannia must've got a vision with too much information, that connected to the aura and created this," said Roderick guardian.

"But what about me? I also had visions as well, just a while ago in Sapphire room," said, Roderick. "Probably God was in your vision, He probably helped you, and besides you didn't get very badly injured as Britannia and Sapphire did." "

Wait I'm confused. What's this, aura?" asked Shquana.

"Each of you have aura give in by God, Sapphire and Britannia aura must have overwhelmed when they been overthinking those vision.

"Guy's this too dangerous; only Jesus will handle this or God. Remember, Roderick would've been like them if God wasn't in the real world." "No, we're not running away. We got to save them," said Allyson.

Down in hell, there was a huge screen that came in front of everyone so that they could see the video.

All: "Huh?" It starts to play, and it was the warriors about to fight Sapphire and Britannia.

Fire saw and was shocked. "Oh, my God. It looks like the visions overwhelmed both Sapphire and Britannia creating that huge aura. That will destroy them, and it will kill anyone that will most likely get in their way.

[GASPED] That's right! Starfire. I can communicate with her to help Sapphire and tell God to make only Julmarie and Sashell get near them. That will break the aura."

"Well, well, well, if it isn't my beautiful Fire." "Go away, Satan Jr. You're really annoying."

"And handsome, right?"

"What do you want?"

"Aren't you watching the fight?"

It showed that Sapphire was attacking each of the Marry Warriors, and Britannia attacking the God and Jesus warriors. They dodged.

"Man, they're fast," said Rihanna. "We have no choice but to fight." Said Junior.

"But that's still our comrade," said Usher.

"But they're under control over that aura," said Abigail.

"Not now, Satan Jr. You know how I am. I don't watch those kinds of fights. Now please leave me alone."

"Fine, see ya. You're missing out on the fun." He left. Fire had a yellow aura and put into an illusion of God.

"God."

"Hello Fire, I know what you're thinking."

"Yes, but you do realize that you need to communicate with Roderick because he's the only one as a God warrior, you gave a vision too in and out of his mind."

"[CHUCKLED] Okay, I'll do that. I just wish that I safe you out of that horrible place, but you want to stay so Satan won't think I made a mistake and think that I'm selfish, and the warriors will save you or most likely Sapphire, huh?"

"Yes."

"Alright, go communicate with Starfire, and I go communicate with Roderick, and don't worry. Roderick aura won't be turned out to be like Sapphire and Britannia's."

"[CHUCKLED]" He disappeared, and Fire woke up. She closes her eye's put her hand together, and she begins to glow blue.

"Starfire, Starfire. Can you hear me.?" Starfire appeared.

"Hey, sis. How's it been?" "Well, not that bad; I'm in hell and all."

"Don't worry; grandpa is helping you. So, I know what you came here for."

"Mmmm....Hmmm... Sapphire."

"I know, I tried to tame the aura, but didn't go anywhere."

"Don't worry, I'm here; let's do this fast before Satan Jr. comes back."

"Ugh, that guy again. He's so annoying."

"I know, but let's do this." They start to glow, and Sapphire fainted, and the aura started to disappear.

"Look at Sapphire," said Josh pointing at her.

Roderick was looking into an illusion and saw a light. "What the...?"

"Roderick."

"That voice, I heard it before."

"I know, I was the boy you saw in your vision. Don't worry; your guardians were right; only Jesus and I can take this, but Sapphire and Britannia did have a vision about both Julmarie and Sashell. I need your help. Can you sprinkle this on both Sashell and Julmarie."

"Yes, of course."

"The reason why I can't do this because they're moving too fast, and I don't want it to end up with everybody, and I can't do everything by myself."

"Yes, of course, God."

"Hurry, Sapphire aura will re-zoomed back. Good luck, Roderick."

Roderick opened his eyes and saw Sapphire's aura about to be re-zoomed. "Julmarie, Sashell, come here!"

"Not now, Roderick!" yelled Sashell.

"Can't you see we're battling!!!" yelled Julmarie, but God gave me this dust to spread on you guys!!" he yelled. Britannia heard, and so did Sapphire; inside Sapphire, the fire disappeared, and Sapphire aura re-appeared.

"Oh no, Fire." Said Starfire.

"UGH!! Really Roderick?" Fire woke up.

"Oh, man." She put her hand on her head. Britannia starts to aim at Roderick. He quickly dodged and started to fly away. Both Sapphire and Britannia were chasing him.

"Oh God. Me and my big mouth. Are they after me?"

"No, they're after the dust," said His guardian.

"What why?" "Because the aura doesn't want to disappear. Remember the aura overwhelmed by the visions." "Oh, oh snap, Britannia is coming closer."

"LOOK OUT, SAPPHIRE!" Sapphire was in front of him. "Roderick over here!" Yelled Usher raising he's hands up. Roderick throws the dust at his cousin, and it overwent him. "Uh-Oh!" He flew towards it; Sapphire went to get it. It was falling towards usher; he was going to capture it, but Sapphire push him out of the way, and she captures it, but Abigail attacked her, and captured it, and flew away, but Britannia used an attack and knocked off Abigail off guard. The dust flew in the air. Both Sapphire and Xavier was heading towards it, but Serena flew in very fast and caught it.

"What am I supposed to do with this?" she asked frighten.

"Sprinkle it over Julmarie and Sashell." said Roderick.

"Oh." Britannia attacked Serena, but junior blocked it, but then Sapphire tackled him in his back. Britannia headed towards Serena, and she flew away. She was right on top of her, Serena quickly through the dust bag and Sheldon captured it, Sapphire quickly attacked Sheldon, but attacked back. The dust flew in the air with a circle around it but then vanished. Each warrior was going to grab it, and so was both Sapphire and Britannia.

Up in heaven in a golden room, looking like a science lab. There was a visual of the fight right now. Somehow Kaguya had a sad face. Jesus noticed.

"Hmm....Kaguya, what's wrong?" asked Jesus, watching the fight on their huge glass bubble showing the fight.

"It's my fault; I should have never given too much information until the time is right. We're supposed to tell them the truth until they received the gem Amethyst, and when they sing the song, that will summon you."

"Don't feel down, Kaguya. Remember, this did happen before."
"Yeah, in the year 1789."

"Don't worry, I can tell that the dust will reach both Sashell and Julmarie, and Fire is doing all her best to help Sapphire calm her out of the aura."

"Thanks, Jesus."

"No problem. By the way, let's see how this fight ends." Down in hell, Satan was laughing so hard.

"Man, this is so funny. Look at this! The warriors were fighting their comrades. Oh, I forgot this really actually happened. It was the year 1789. HAHAHAHAHAHAHAHAH!!!!!"
He put his hand over he's the eye's still laughing. "See! And God is not doing anything." Said Satan Jr. coming in.

"Of course, he's selfish, and didn't he said he treats his warrior's kind, while you treat your demons horribly?" asked Lucifer Jr. coming in.

"What the fuck is this, then."

"Oh, by the way.... Have you noticed fire lately? She seems so quiet, closing her eye's all the time."

"Who cares, she's stuck in hell forever, and God got nothing to do with it."

"Oh, okay, well, I'm going to go watch the fight. Satan Jr., you are coming?"

"Yeah." They both left. Upon earth in Sapphire and Britannia's house, the mothers were worried about their children.

"Man, I've haven't heard about our children."

"Yeah, it been 1 hour later, they should have come back by the way," said Julmarie's mother.

"Forget about the food, it was a huge explosion over there," said Sapphire, Britannia, Sashell, Roderick, Rihanna aunty Neata.

"I think we need to go over there and see what's up," said Josh's mother.

"Yeah, let's go," said Lisa.

"But my car won't hold, let one car go, and like three women go.

"For an instant, me, Lisa and Neata go," said Yanique.

"Good idea." Said Selena and Cory's mom.

"But wait, you said your car wouldn't hold," said Re-Re mother.

"They can walk. We'll be right back. Still, cook dinner." The three girls left. They went to the car and drive to the grocery store.

On the battlefield, all of them were about to grab the dust, but luckily Cory got it. "Yes." Sapphire got very angry and attacked him, but he dodged it, Britannia was behind him.

"Cory, behind you," said Winston, pointing out. He turned around and Britannia kicked him, the dust went right out of his hands and Britannia caught it, but Rihanna used a flower bomb on Britannia back and the dust fell. The car came, the three women go out of the car.

"I don't see them," said Lisa.

"[GASPED] BUT I SEE THE WARRIORS!!!!!LOOK!!!!!," yelled Neata.

"But their glowing."

"Of course, they don't want to show off their identity probably," said Yanique.

Sashell and Julmarie noticed Lisa, Neata, and Yanique. "Oh snap, Julmarie look!" pointed out Sashell.

"Oh no, we must be gone too long. They must've been worried and come and search for us," said Julmarie. The dust came headed towards Yanique.

"Oh no, it's heading towards your mom." Yanique noticed and captured it.

"Huh? What is that?" asked Neata.

"What do you think it is? It's dust." Britannia and Sapphire came rushing over towards Yanique. She saw Sashell and Julmarie coming her way and she spread it only towards them." Then they both begin to glow. Everyone, including both Sapphire and Britannia, stare at them. Sashell had a yellow dress, and Julmarie had a red tuxedo. They were glowing. As soon as they open their eyes, Sashell has yellow eye's and Julmarie had red. The dust disappeared.

"Whoa, this is what you mean, Roderick?" asked Roman.

"Yes, even God came to my visions before. He gave me that dust, and they look good."

"Yeah, they do." Up in heaven in the science lab, Both Kaguya and Jesus was watching. "Oh my.... Wow."

"See, I told you not to worry." "Wait, are you telling me that..."

"Yup, it was fire idea," said God light coming in.

"Wow, fire is very smart."

"Indeed."

"Now, let's see how Satan and his son's like it now before you ask why it's because he's playing on the big screen."

"Oh, I see. [CHUCKLED]" Down in hell, all of the people in that place, including Satan's son's mouth was huge.

"What the......... FUCK!!??" yelled Satan Jr. "B-But HOW!!!!??" Asked Lucifer Jr., Fire was so happy and had a big smile on her face.

"Like I said. Never underestimate God and the warriors." She whispered. The whole place was shaking. Everyone was talking at once. "Uh-Oh..." "Dad...." "FFFFUUUUUUUUUUUUUUUUUUCCCKKKK!!!!!!!!!!!!!!!!!!!!!! !!!!!!!!!!!!!!!," yelled Satan all the way from his office.

"[CHUCKLED]. That what Satan gets for underestimate God."

In Satan's office, He was throwing stuff around.

"Ugh, I thought this was going to be true, but no. Why?! Why can't God lose for ONCE!!!!!?????? [SIGH]. Well let's see how this battle goes." Upon earth at the battlefield, Sapphire and Britannia were in shocked, looking at both Sashell and Julmarie.

"What is this?" asked Julmarie.

"To be honest. I kind of like this outfit. What's is this?" asked Sashell.

"It was the dust," said Roderick coming to them. "What do you mean by that?" "He means that both Sapphire and Britannia had visions of both of you. You two have the power to break the aura seal," said Sashell guardian.

"Oh, I see, well we got to do it fast. Before they strike down our mother's."

"Alright. Let's do this." They went close to them. Sapphire and Britannia were going to attack them by using their powers, but

Sashell and Julmarie both yelled, stop putting out their hand. They both stopped.

Both: "[GROANS]!!!" They start to lay down and close their eyes. Some electric start to came on their bodies. Sapphire had the same vision as the boy. Britannia had the same vision as the female. The aura became increase. It starts to bind at each other, then creating a dragon.

"Oh my God!" yelled Allyson.

"We got to protect, Neata, Yanique, and Lisa!!" yelled Junior.

They all went to them and created a force field. "Oh my," said Lisa.

"Okay, now we really need to be more careful and stronger against this now," said Sashell.

Six

THE STRENGTH

G reat now a dragon?" asked Roderick.

"Like I said, we need to be more careful and stronger against this now," said Sashell.

"Hey, where are the warriors?" asked Julmarie. "

They're leading the people into safety." Answered Roderick.

"Well, at least the aura is out of both Sapphire and Britannia."

"Yeah which turn into that," replied Sashell. The dragon starts to attack them, but they dodged very quickly.

"Whoa! That was close." Said Roderick in a heart rush.
"Man, this dragon is going to be tuff."

"Again, I'm going to say this if you didn't understand we got to be careful," said Sashell.

"Okay, Sashell, we heard you the first time," said Julmarie.

"Really? The first time?"

"Oh look, Poor Sapphire and Britannia just lying there." With electric in them. The Dragon blew out flames out of its mouth. Each of them dodged really quickly. "Fire breath? Great, he can breathe out fire breath? Oh, we're screwed." Said Julmarie.

Sashell flew down and struck its tail using an explosion star. The dragon screamed, and Sashell flew away. It breathes out the fire, and it hit her.

Both: "SASHELL!!!" As soon as the fire disappeared, she had a yellow force field around her.

"Oh, thank God." "We need to fight too."

"Yeah." They start to use their powers, and they also hit the dragon. It hit it, and it begins to scream. It quickly turned around to both of them, but they start to fly separated ways. Sashell joined in, and each used their attacks flying around hitting it. It screamed, and echoes begin to vibrate, and it sends them flying while covering their ears. They both landed.

"Ah!! What a powerful scream," said Roderick.

"Even echo screams. What kind of power does this dragon have?" asked Julmarie. It came flying up to them and it used sunbeam.

All 3: "Sapphire's move attack??!! LOOK OUT!!!"

They went three separate ways. The dragon starts to aim at Roderick; he kept flying very fast and flew into a brick wall. He used his electricity to the wall so that the sunbeam won't destroy it. Julmarie was quickly behind it and used an orange beam, and it hit on the back of its head. It turned around quickly and used sun beamed, but he dodged it. Sashell came and used star bombs on its stomach, and it screamed.

In the ally, the warriors were above the people leading them back to safety.

"Man, how much people are there?" asked Tristan.

"You really want to fight the dragon, do you?" asked Rihanna. "Yeah. They're fighting a dragon while I'm evacuating the slower people."

"Remember, you got to protect them, Tristan." Said Josh.

"Alright, Alright, but I want to strike my fire powers to that dragon."

"I hope Britannia and Sapphire doing well," said Trishawna.

"Alright, this way. This way. Here's an ally so you won't be near the fight." Said Junior. The people ran toward that ally; even cars drove up to that ally.

"I've got an idea," said Re-Re. "What is it?" asked Selena. "How about some of us, go help them over there, and some stay here and guide the people away from the battlefield."

"Great idea," said Shquana.

"Okay, since Julmarie is a marry warrior, Roderick is a God warrior and Sashell is a guardian, since there are only three guardians Sapphire, Britannia, and Sashell is, but both Sapphire and Britannia are down, that means only three Jesus warriors can go, two marry warriors and two God warriors. Agreed?" said Junior.

ALL: "Agreed." "So, who Jesus wants to go."

All: "ME!!" "Whoa, that's a rush."

"Hey, Don't Roderick control both water and lightning? So, I don't think Abigail and Roman shouldn't go," said Xavier.

"BE QUIET XAVIER!!" they both yelled.

"True, true, so Abigail and Roman your stay."

Both: "Oh my."

"Hey, we need to help the people. So, I think they need Usher because of his wind powers. E.J with he's ice powers, and Tristan with he's fire powers, so I think that's up to the fight. Now the Marry warriors Selena and Serena, just them."

"What do you mean by only them?" asked Winston.

"Because they're both girls, have the same similar names and their good in combat."

"We need more boys; let me go," said Josh.

"Whatever. Now the God warriors. How about Hmmmm.... How about Meisha and Allyson."

"You can't send my niece out there," said Shquana. "Shquana, we're the warriors. We don't even know we're related or not. So, Allyson, you go."

76

"Yeah. Don't worry about me aunty Shquana. I'll be fine."

"Alright." "Alright, scatter." They left. Up in heaven in the golden science lab. They were watching the fight from above. Jesus was smiling. Kaguya turned around and asked.

"Jesus, what's so funny?" The warriors don't stand a chance against that thing."

"Oh yes, they would," said Michael Danderson coming up flying.

"Mmm.... It looks like you know, Michael," said Jesus.

"Well, God did send me the envelope to Kaguya. According to plan."

"Wait. What? What do you mean according to the plan? I'm confused."

"Well, since the messiah wants me to tell you, based on the look in his eyes, I'll tell you. Well, the fire was communicating with Starfire and had a good idea, she asked if she could test the warrior's strength to see if they're strong enough. You do know if God asks Satan to help with the warriors with their strength, he'll disagree because he's evil?"

Fire told God to tell me and send this envelope to you about giving Britannia and Sapphire visions to help them out after their very bad injuries from protecting the marry warriors as they were in human form and didn't know they were the marry warrior.

Fire decided to choose both Sapphire and Britannia because they had a vision of both Sashell, your warrior, and possibly the guardian of the comment and Julmarie guardian of Eris and possibly can become the guardian of the sun since Eris orbit came directly from the sun, They rest not. If only the other Kaguya warriors/Guardians appeared. If they had visions, it could only work on Kaguya warriors because Kaguya was born human, while Jesus was born in heaven and born again on earth Marry Warriors can even have this, but Their just new to this and didn't have a vision, not even Roderick can have this. Fire knows this is risky and didn't want you to know Kaguya. Because you'll refuse, so She told God to trick you and made you give Sapphire and Britannia too many visions, even dough they weren't ready for the truth yet until they get the gem, Ruby.

After the aura been released, but God is controlling it; God even told Rodrick that to sprinkle this dust over Sashell and Julmarie because that's the only way that the aura can come out of both Britannia and Sapphire because they saw them in the visions. This is only a test, to test out their strength so to see if their strong enough so that we won't help them all the time. Like their last few fights."

"Wow, it seems like the king of popstar music has a good memory," said Jesus.

"[CHUCKLED]" "Oh, so this is a test?" Both:

"Yup."

"Wait ain't Satan playing this on a big screen in front of everyone, to look like God is a terrible man, remember fire told us."

"He thinks God is treating his warriors like this but doesn't realize this is a test," said Jesus.

"Oh, okay, I thought. This was real. Wait, who's going to tell the warriors?"

"Ida will."

"Serita other triplets, huh? Well, I don't blame her. She's perfect. It is thanks to Serita that Sashell and Julmarie transformed."

"Indeed. That is the team's guardian angel, anyways," said Michael.

A little girl came up with cookies. "Aww, how cutie."

"[CHUCKLED] MJ king of pop, I love your music."

"He-He." "Oh, I remember. During the warrior's previous days, they always listen to music Michael," said Kaguya.

"Yeah, they say I was a legendary superstar singer."

"Don't worry Michael, One day you'll achieve by summoning your holy swords that I implanted in you, and you'll be able to go to earth fight with warriors and see your family members, even dough it been six years."

"They'll remember me Jesus, like the whole world, thinks of you at church, pray to you, and love you."

"Well, back when I was alive, people say you were a second Jesus Michael," said the little girl.

"That's because I love Jesus. And says that I love everyone traveled around the world as Jesus did."

"[CHUCKLED]." "What you are here, for.... What's your name?" "Shelly."

"What you are doing here, Shelly?"

"Cookie. I made them myself in the kitchen." The three of them grabbed a cookie and ate it.

"Hmmm... This is delicious.

What kind is it?" "Chocolate chip."

"Well back in the Jewish days, Jesus and I never have these."

"Well, everything belongs to the Jews," said Jesus.

"Well, I hope that fire is okay in hell," said Michael.

"Don't worry. She's safe; God's aura is surrounding her. Well, I wonder how Satan face will be after they even beat the dragon. Wait, didn't this happen in the year 1789?"

"Well, not exactly. It was a dragon sent by Satan, but the warriors defeated it."

"I heard they hardly do," said Shelly.

"True it was." Down in hell, Satan was laughing his ass off.

"Man, can this day get any good or what?" Lucifer Jr. came in.

"What up, dad, still watching the fight?"

"Hell yeah. Are you?"

"Nah, I'm busy roasting and carving people. From their stomach."

"Oh, no wonder why I heard people screaming. Keep it down; I'm enjoying this fight.

"[SIGH] Whatever, I soon have seen the fight, if I'm done. If I'm done too late, tell me how the fight ended."

"Whatever. And close the door while you're leaving, BUT!" He turned around.

"What is it?" Aren't the people in shocked, about how God treating his warriors?"

"Well, before I left, people were in shocked."

"Oh, good Good!!! FUCKING GOOOOOOOOODDDDD!!!!!!!!!!"

"Well, I'm out of here." He shut the door. Fire was in her cell with yellow aura flowing in her. She was contacting God. "God...God.... God..." She stopped, and the aura disappeared. Satan Jr. came.

"Yo, what's up, my wifey?"

"I wouldn't be your wifey if you were the last boy on earth."

"Aw, looks like someone is Mad."

"Mad? Mad about what?"

"God is doing this to the warriors."

"No, I'm not. You don't know God, even if he's your father creator." Satan Jr.'s eyes became red in flames.

"Shut the hell up."

"Well, go away. I don't want anything to do with you," he said as he left the room finally.

"Make sure." She looked around to make sure that Satan Jr. was nowhere in sight. She didn't even trace his sent.

"Finally. Now back where I was. God..." Yellow aura came on her, she closed her eyes and visualized her in a bright room.

"God? God." A light shine appeared from above.

"Hello fire, why don't you call me the other name?"

"Because I'm not fit to call you that for choosing to be in hell believing that the warriors going to save me, even if I'm in this room, this beautiful bright room."

"Don't say it like that. Remember, in 1990, the warriors were willing to save you but been reborn."

"Yeah, by telling you to make them be reborn because they were willing to go to hell to save me, but it will be a trap, and I don't want them to be in the same way that I have."

"You are a very brave girl like- "

"Please don't say it like that."

"You are very brave like Jesus and Kaguya. Soon Sapphire will be in the next step, and so will Starfire." "[CHUCKLED]"

Seven

TRISTAN

Tristan was in a dark room. "Huh? What's going on? Where am I?" Then the room started to change into blue flames then a field then a kingdom. "What is this? Guys? Anyone? HELLO!!!" Then it showed people walking past him, but the people had blue skin. "What the heck is going on here?" Then they all started to be in huge shocked looking above seeing their kind glowing. "Huh? Who is that?" Then the illusion stopped. He heard footsteps approaching and he begins to back up. Then he bumped into someone and it was a man completely covered in a white glow.

"Hello, Tristan."

"W-Who are you...?"

"You'll find out really soon. You'll need this. Good luck." He vanished.

"Wait, what is this orb? Hey?" He woke up sweating.

"What the heck." Then his airy appeared.

"Something wrong, Tristan?"

"Uh...Yeah. I had a dream. A dream I was in some blue fire field, and a glowing man appeared. He gave me something. Like an orb." The fairy was a little shocked.

"Do you know who he is?"

"Uh...I think it's time for school..."

"Don't try to dodge the question. Who is he?"

"Tristan! Let's go. You're almost late."

"This isn't over Fire Fairy." He got up and got ready. He and his siblings reached the bus and sat down.

"Ugh, Midterms. I hate those," says Usher.

"Well it is the middle of Fall, I thought those started like January or March," says E.J.

"It's going to start different they said and begin it in September," says Roman.

"Something wrong, Tristan? You're not this quiet," says Abigail.

"It's just. I had a dream last night. A weird one."

"{GASPED] You mean a vision dream. Be careful. You might be like Sapphire and Britannia," says Sonny.

"It's not only that, I more concern which was that man." "A man visits you?" asked Gabriella.

"This isn't a great time to disgusted it on the bus, people can hear us." Then a girl with a group approached.

"Hey there, losers, you're sitting on our spot."

"You're spot? LOL, No one has any spot on this bus."

"Until we came." Says another girl. "Hello, Tristan." They all said at the same time. "We can allow you to stay here, but your siblings just have to go."

"Why won't you make us?" Says Roman seeing he was ready to fight. Everyone got their attention seeing if they're really going to fight.

"EY! Roman. You don't hit girls," says Sonny grabbing his shoulder.

"Well, we can't rely on both Gabriella and Abigail to defeat all 4 of them."

"And you're willing to hit a girl? We'll just be mature and move, taking Tristan with us," says Sonny. They got up and move to a different seat.

"Girls, I got a mission for one of you." They were now at the school. They arrived, getting their breakfast.

"Okay. We're here; no one can bother us here. So, what's up?" asked Roman.

"So, you see-" One of the girls started to overhear their conversation and was a little shocked.

"Wait, so you had a dream of that. In my opinion, I think it was Jesus trying to tell you that the demons are going to attack soon."

"But what this orb means, and I can't find it."

"It will come out when the battlefield is out, but for now, let's focus on school and keep an eye out," said Gabriella. "Wait, did your fairy had something to do with this?"

"No, and I asked him, and he dodged the question. I'll ask when it's break time." The bell rang and they all got ready for the first period. The girl ran to her crew.

"Guys, you wouldn't believe what I just heard." So, she started to explain the story.

"You've got to be kidding me?"

"No, it's the truth."

"They can't be the worriers; you didn't see Roman try to hit me? You think a warrior will do that?"

"We need more evidence. After the first period, I will stalk them and see what's up." In the first period, Tristan started to act a little strange and lean his head on his arm. He started to have flashbacks as he was in the same field.

"What is this? This field again...That light...It has a man inside of it...What is he doing? Why am I here? What the...HELL!!!" He shouted as he stands up, and everyone was staring at him.

"Oh shit."

"Tristan, there's no need for cursing in my class, as for that go and see the principal," ordered the teacher.

"Yes..." He left. One of the girls started to get suspicious, and as soon as Tristan left, she asked a question.

"Miss, I'm not feeling so great may I please go to the nurse?"

"And what is it, you're not feeling so well?"

"My stomach. May I please go?"

"Sure." She steps aside from the room and begins to stalk Tristan. Tristan just left the principal office and reached to his locker.

"Okay, the coast is clear." He opened his locker and summoned his fairy.

"What can I do for you warrior of the fire." 'I want answers. I know you know it. Who was that man who gave me that orb, and who was those people in a blue fire kingdom?"

"Uh..."

"Don't try to dodge the question because you know. What is going on!"

"Tristan!"

Not so loud. "Thanks to you, I got an hour of detention because I was thinking about it. Also, there was some guy on some light like he was dying to tell me about."

"Tristan...Us Fairies aren't supposed to tell you just yet."

"Yet?" "AH-HA!"

BOTH: "HUH?" The fairy quickly vanished.

"What the- Elizabeth?"

"So, one of my friends was right; you are a warrior? What type of warrior." "That's none of your business."

"I guess the whole school will love to know about your little secret."

"Do you have proof?"

"I'm the most popular girl in school. Of course, they'll believe me."

"I doubt it, what I got to do?"

"Make me a warrior."

"I can't do that."

"Fine looks like everyone will know your secret."

"Ugh." In Hell, Satan was spying on Tristan on what's going on with him.

"So, it looks like the warrior of fire is having some teenage drama. And she looks mean. She looks like she got the lying sin."

"Plus, she's on the list father," says Lucifer Jr., arriving.

"Send the demons to capture her." He nodded his head and vanished. He called God on his crystal orb, and he answered. "God, What the hell is going on with Tristan?"

"That's none of your concern, Satan."

"Oh, it is, I'm going to be... Truthful. He's almost like me; he's the God of fire."

"Don't say one of my son's warriors are ever like you." Then Satan started to shake.

"Ugh, what the hell? Did you used Reality bending on me?!"

"Nope."

"Damn you!!!" He yelled as Hell shake and crumbled.

"Just wait! Just wait until I come out of here."

"We'll see." He hangs up the projector.

"Damn that man. I just need the lying sin, then Sapphire, and I'm complete." Lucifer Jr. arrived where the demons are.

"Demons. We found a new target. It's a girl named Elizabeth. She goes to Hartford High. Find and see if she has the lying sin."

"Yes, your majesty." He vanished and so did they. At the school, Elizabeth and Tristan were still arguing.

"Just go away, Elizabeth. You're really bugging me. "Hmph." She walked away.

"Wait until everyone sees, and I caught it all on tape. Then she came across a dark girl who appeared out of nowhere in a corner. \

"Whoa, what the hell? Uh, who are you?"

"I heard what happened."
"What?"
"With Tristan. Did you know Tristan had a secret Diary."?

"Why didn't you bring it?"

"It has a lock and it's open to Tristan's voice. You got his voice on tape."

"Uh...Yeah."

"Come with me."

"Damn, now everyone's going to know my secret."

"Demons! Demons!" "Demon, where?"

"It's very close! It's like it's in this hallway."

"The hallway? Now. [GASPED] Elizabeth!" He started to run away.

"Wait Tristan..." The fairy started to follow him. He arrived in the hallway and spotted Elizabeth walking with an unknown girl.

"ELIZABETH!!!"

"Huh?" Both of them were in shock.

"Don't go near her. She's a demon!"

"What?" "Looks like I have no choice." She attacked Elizabeth by ripping her heart out.

"[GASPED]." Gasped Tristan in shocked.

Eight

TRISTAN PART II

"Damn you! Fire Fairy!" He nodded and they transformed. He charged straight at the demon, but then more demon arrived. It was Lois and Lucy. He backed up. The demon girl revealed her identity and it was Jade. She checked the heart, and it showed no dark spot. "No sin, guess I have to dispose of you."

"No!!" He shot out a fire at them, But Aleg and Peter arrived and blocked it with their moves.

"You're outnumbered, give up." He still started to shoot out fire, but they kept blocking it. "This is sad; it seems like something is distracting you." Jade was about to squeeze the heart, but she been attacked from behind a lighting attack. She crashed out the window.

"Need a hand Tristan?" Asked Abigail is appearing with the other Jesus warriors.

"I'll protect Elizabeth until Sapphire, and the other comes." The rest arrived outside attacking Jade, but she used to protect, but it broke.

"Damn it!" Tristan then got up and followed the demons who were going to attack his siblings off guard as they were attacking Jade. They got hit.

"Damn you." They attack him, but he was dodging, but Barley. He then used a shield, but then it cracked and broke. He crashed down to the roof ceiling, but he quickly got up. Two demons were coming after him, but Sonny created rock boulders and hit them with it. Tristan looked at his younger brother, and he gave him a thumbs up. Tristan got up but went back down.

"What is going on with me? I feel so weak...Damn." He watches as his siblings are fighting the demons.

"My powers...What's going... Is it because of...of that dream...?" He fainted. They were all in shock about what happened to him, and the demons were going to attack him, but Abigail used the Water force field.

"Damn...Tristan! Get up! What's up? I can't hold this out any longer and the victim is dying, where are you guys?" Another demon arrived above her and threw a dark ball above her.

"Damn! Tristan!" Then another attack collided with it, and it was Sashell.

"Don't worry; we're here." Says Josh.

"Thank goodness."

"Damn, now we're outnumbered. Aleg went straight for Sashell, but she used to protect. She flew above him, and Britannia was in front of him blasting an attack, and Sashell kicked him to it.

"AH!" He yelled. The demons were throwing dark clouds at them, but they seem to be dodging.

"There's Sapphire! Grab her."

"Not so fast!" yelled Xavier as he blasted beams at them. They got hit. Sapphire flew to the victim, where sonny was protecting.

"Thanks, Sonny." Sapphire Started to heal the victim.

"Who is she."

"Her name is Elizabeth, and she got attacked by the demons, it seems since she's the most popular girl in school, Satan had an interest in her if she had the lying sin."

"Oh, I see, looks like he's going after people who are mean." He nodded his head.

"There she's healed, but we got to get her out of here."

"Attention everyone! Attention, the warriors are battling outside so no one is allowed to be in the hallway until further notice."

"Well looks like no one's going to be in danger."

"I'm going to Tristan. She flew towards him. As soon she was flying towards him, she got attacked and crashed to the building floor.
"Ugh." "Listen up, Sapphire you need to come with us."

"Never!" Then Roman attack him with his lightning bolt.

"I got him, Sapphire. You healed the victim?"

"Yes, but I got to heal Tristan keep fighting them off." She flew up to the ceiling.

"Tristan? Tristan?" He was woken up a bit.

"Sapphire...?" "What happened to you?"

"I keep having dreams and flashbacks. Almost like what happened to both you and Britannia."

"I need to heal you, don't go through that pain on what happened to us."

"No, Sapphire, I just need answers."

"But-" "No." He touched her a bit then felt something.

"Huh? What was that?" He grabbed Sapphire's hand, and in front of them, it started to glow and glow brighter. Everyone stopped what they were doing and was in huge shocked with is that?" Asked Junior.

"It's starting to feel hot now, extremely hot!" says Ally.

"Could this be the orb he was talking about?" asked Roman.

"Sapphire..." "Hmm...Tristan, what is this?"

"This is what he gave me."

"This orb?" He placed it inside of him, and he glowed blue with flames and flew up.

"Everyone ducks...." He blasted a huge flame thrower at them demons. They crashed hard and all of them were in shock.

"OMG! Damn!" Says Monica. The demons were badly injured. In Hell, Satan was also in shock.

"What the-Is this what God did? Put something in that child. No, it has to be Sapphire doing, but- Ugh."

"It's time to get rid of you Demons once and for all" But then they vanished.

"Seems like they couldn't take it and went away." Says Serena.

Tristan collapse and fall. The power just vanished from him as he was falling.

ALL: "TRISTAN!" Abigail created a soft water bubble to soften his fall. They all flew down towards him.

"Hey! Are you alright?" Asked Josh.

"Huh? What-What happened?"

"You kicked the demon's ass, that's what happened. That huge flame thrower was really big. OMG." Says Selena.

"How did you contain that power?" asked Sheldon.

"Like I said before, I had a dream, and some guy covered in white gave me an orb. My dream was about me in some kingdom of blue fire with people. I then saw a huge light and a man was inside of it. I was then a guy with white light covered gave me an orb."

"I think Ida will have something to do with it, like now," says Sashell. "And ditch School?"

"You can't go back; people are going to see your identity."

"Also, when I touched Sapphire, it reappeared."

"And they're after me. For what?"

"I think Ida will answer it, let's go to my sister's house or any house that's near here."

"My house it's near," says Roderick.

"Is Narda at work?"

"Yes, nobody seems to be home."

"Alright, let's go there and summon Ida." They flew off. And was already at her house.

"Let's go to the Grouje," says Rihanna. They entered and de-transformed. "Ida? Ida?" She appeared.

"I'm here."

"Ida, we need to ask you something."

"No need I watched the whole fight. It's because he touched Sapphire which the orb appeared. Sapphire also has fire powers; you know the cause of the sun."
"But what about that man I saw in my dream, actually. I saw a man who was in some type of light-catching everyone's

96

attention. I saw another man, but he was in pitch white like I don't know his identity, like us, so the human won't know who we are or understand us. Who is he?"

"That's Jesus Christ." ALL: "WHAT?!"

"Jesus Christ came to visit me. But-Fire fairy," he appeared.

"I'm sorry, I was even told by Jesus not to told you...yet."

"That's all you guys asked me for, huh?"

"Then why didn't Jesus told you to tell him?" asked Shquana.

"He just told me to tell you guys. Don't worry; you guys will also meet him, very son. Now then. You should go back; everything is back to normal. God put everything back to normal."

"Wait, what about that orb. What was that?" "It's the orb of Fire; you'll understand once the time has come." She says as she vanished. "Well, we better get to school since we got our answer," says Britannia. "Damn..." 'I wonder...When could I meet Jesus?' Thought he was roman in his head.

Nine

ROMAN

The Jesus warriors flew back to school in each bathroom seeming like they were in the bathroom, and they walked to class. "I wonder what the demons are going to plan for us now?" Usher said.

"We have to wait and see." Says Roman. 'And I have to train to get strong like Tristan.' A few hours have passed, and they were already home. "I wonder what mom is cooking today?"

"There you are; do you know how late it is?" asked their stepdad?"

"Eric, it's 3:30. We're fine." "Not you, to my kids?" "But what about our sibling's dad?" asked Gabriella.

"I don't care." "Where's mom?"

"She's out and left me to cook."
ALL: "UGH!" "What? You don't like my cooking?" "To be honest... Hell no," says Usher.

"What the... Why?" "Eric, you put too much salt; we like our mothers cooking," says Abigail.

"Well, too bad, I'm cooking." "Thank goodness I have money. You'll want some McDonalds?" asked Tristan.

ALL: "Sure." "E.J. and Gabriella, you stay here?"

"They can come with us!" says Sonny.

"My children, my responsibility!"

"Guys, just go."

"No way, fine we'll.... stay," says Roman. They entered the house and to the Romans' room.

"God, I wish he wasn't our stepdad."

"But guys, without him. I wouldn't even exist." Says E.J. "Neither will I.," says Gabriella.

"Well, we are warriors; we can just fly our way there." Suggested Abigail.

"No, then Eric will wonder where we at and assume we sneak out, and E.J. and Gabriella will get punished." Explain Sonny.

"That's true." "Hey, Tristan. You said you met Jesus Christ, right?' "

That's what Ida said. Why?"

"I wonder, who was that man you saw in some light in some blue fire kingdom."

"I have no idea."

"I'll be right back," says Roman walking out.

"Where are you going?"

"To the bathroom." He reached and summoned his fairy.

"Fairy of lighting, who is the guy that was in some light in a fire kingdom."

"We can't tell. We don't have permission."

"Well, I need answers. I'm going to train my lighting powers because I felt so useless in the last fight."

"What are you talking about? You saved Sapphire's life from being captured." "They said they need Sapphire, why?"

"For Satan's plan to come out of hell."

"That means I really got to practiced. Let's transform." They transformed, and he flew out to the sky.

"Damn not enough clouds, if only I have Sapphire with me or Tristan's firepower to heat the water, turning it to more clouds. I'll use what I got." He started to spiral lighting all over the sky and used the clouds as his enemies for practiced. At Tristan's room, the siblings were gossiping until a call from Sashell came.

"Looks like they want us at Aunty Serita's house. Let's go," says Usher.

"But what about Roman?' asked Gabriella.

"I'll go look." Says Sonny walking out. He reached the bathroom and knocked on the door.

"Roman come on, we got to go to Aunty Serita's house, everyone's there." But there was no reply. "Roman?" The door was unlocked, and he opened it, and his older brother wasn't there.

"Roman?" He reached back to the room. "Uh, guys? Romans not here?"

"We can assume he left. I'll leave him a voice message, let's go." They summoned a portal to the house, and they went through it and were at the home.

"Hey guys, uh, where's roman?" Asked Josh.

"He's somewhere, but I left him a voice message," says Tristan.

"Are we going to summon Ida for some deeds about the demons?" asked Trishawna.

"But it wouldn't be the same without Roman," says Ally.

"I think I know where he's at," says Sashell.

"Oh, yeah? Where?"

"Take a look in the sky." She says, pointing up. They went through the window and was in shocked, seeing lighting all over the sky.

"What is he doing? He's catching everyone's attention," says Shquana.

"I'll take care of it. Venus of fairy." She was summoned, and they transformed.

"I'll come with you," says Britannia.

"Tristan let's help Roman," says Sapphire. He nodded and grabbed her hand.

"Julmarie?"

"Of course." He grabbed her hand and they begin to glow. The sun started to heat the water, and clouds started kicking in.

"What the-? Sapphire!" says Britannia. They stopped.

"I think Roman is training after seeing what happened to you, Tristan," says Julmarie.

"Why would he do that? He needs some orb that Jesus gave me," replied Jesus. In the sky, Roman started to concentrate, and lighting started to appear from his body. Both Sashell and Britannia appeared from the clouds.

"Roman." "CHA!!" He released a huge amount of lighting power from him, and it hit Britannia while Sashell quickly used Shield.

"AHH!" Yelled Britannia as she was hit.

"Britannia!!" Yelled Sashell. Roman was shocked, and the clouds vanished by the static. She fell.

"No, he said when he was about to fly to catch his cousin, but then Junior caught her flying up with Sapphire, Tristan, and Allyson.

"What the Heck Roman, you're training cause what happened to me?" "Not just that, I just felt useless in the last fight."

"No, you weren't. You saved me from that demon." In Hell, Satan was watching them through the crystal orb. "So, I see looks like the God of lighting is disappointed, and not all the warriors aren't there. Demons!" They arrived. "This is the chance to get Sapphire; I'm going to give you something, cause watching that last fight, Tristan powers wore out. You'll have a chance. Just hit Sapphire with this and her powers will be weakened. There're only six warriors and there's 10 of you, you'll stand a chance. Keep on the low, and you only have one chance." They nodded, and Lois token the orb power and they teleported. "Father, you do realize; you gave them the wrong power." Says Lucifer Jr.

"What do you mean, boy?"

"That's the power to weaken their fairy not their power." "Well, once she's human, she's defenseless, and boom, you have your girl." says Satan Jr. arriving.

"Well, that does make sense. Don't you got fire to attend to?"

"Yeah." He vanished and so did his brother. On earth, the remaining warriors were talking to Roman.

"Dude, it's okay, besides we're waiting so we can talk to Ida. You'll get that power too, and you're not useless. No one is." Says Sapphire. Roman spotted a demon above her, and he blasted something at her.

"Look out!!" Yelled Roman as he blocked the attack. He was covered in dark static and fall. "ROMAN!!" yelled Sapphire as she tries to reach out to him but has to quickly back up as an attacker tries to hit her. Roman was falling for his life but then woken up.

"What the hell. My body...It feels weird. Like, weaken." Then he de-transformed into his human form. His fairy was weakened, and he quickly caught him.

"Lighting? LIGHTING? What happened to you?!"

"I'm....weaken...This is one of...."

"Of whom?" "Satan's power."

"He was in shocked." "No way...! How can I fix this? Ida?"

"No.... [PAINITING]...Jesus..?" He was shocked.

"How? We're falling to our deaths here, and the warriors up there are busy fighting off the demons."

"I'll try to communicate." Then he passed out. "Lighting? Lighting?! HELP!!!!!!" He called out as he was falling. He soon reached the ground, but then a light appeared and caught him, taking him to the woods and landed.

"Huh? I'm alive?" He looked up and saw a man carrying him.

"Hello, Roman?" "Huh? GASPED]." It was Jesus Christ. "No...No way." "I'll heal your fairy so you can fight with the warriors."

"But what about the other ones?"

"They're about to fight, like right now." He healed out his hand to heal the fairy, and he passed it to him.

"Jesus, I will like to ask you something."

"No need, I know."

Ten

ROMAN PART II

Jesus started to heal the fairy, and it was in good health. "Thank you, uh...I know what I did was embarrassing, but..."

"No, it wasn't. You just want to be like your brother. Here's the orb of lighting."

"Thank you, but before I placed it in, I need to touch you. Tristan said something about a man he saw."

"Of course." He held out his hand and Roman touched it and then he started to have visions. He was in a lightning kingdom. Over a Castle with a woman and a man, it suddenly cut to a scene where a man was in a light over the kingdom.

"What are these?" Then Jesus Let go. "Jesus?"

"It's not time yet. Right now, you have to help the warriors. We'll meet again real soon." He disappeared. Roman had the orb in his hand.

"Fairy of Lighting, are you in good health?"

"Of course."

"Now, let's go help the warriors." In the house, the other warriors spotted the warriors fighting in the sky.

"Look the warriors are in trouble. Let's transform," says Winston. They transformed and flew up to the sky.

"Damn, more are coming."

"No need, we'll just attack some random person," says Jade. She flew down. Zack started to blast beams at Sashell, but she was dodging by flying to the left. She was then across and zoom at him warp speed and punched him, then kicked him in the face towards down, but then, he quickly grabbed her feet as they were falling. She was blasting beams at his face, but then he injured her leg by using a dark beam.

"Ugh!" He then appeared from the smoke blast and punched her.

"Ugh!" She then was flipping down trying to gain her balance, but then Sheldon grabbed her. "Thanks, Sheldon.

"Oh no, you don't!" Then Winston blasted a red beam towards him, and he got injured. Jade reached down and spotted a woman walking with her baby. "HA!" "[SCREAMED]!" Then Sapphire used the shield to protect the woman and her child.

"Damn you, Sapphire."

"Go on."

"Thank you, warrior." She started to run with her baby. Jade started to fly away to find the next person. Sapphire followed. 'Yeah, keep following me, Sapphire.' She spotted men waiting for the bus. She attacked him, but he dodged, but then a car was coming, but then Julmarie grabbed him really quickly.

"Oh, God, thank you." Julmarie nodded. Jade started to fly away, and Sapphire continue to follow. Julmarie set the man down and followed Sapphire. Jade was in the middle of the woods and landed.

"Nowhere left to hide, Jade."

"Yeah, for you! NOW!" A pair of hands came almost grabbing Sapphire, but then Julmarie came and quickly grabbed her.

"Ugh! NO!!" "You'll never capture her, Demon." She started to fly away.

"We need to follow her; she's going to attack innocent people.

"Alright, let's go." They followed her. Jade reached to a man who's working on a building. "HA!" The men spotted her and were in shock.

BOTH: "NO!" They reached out, but then Lighting came, and Jade was badly injured.

"AH!!" "Huh?" Then Roman with ultimate power appeared. "Be gone, demon!" He says as lighting came out of his hand full power, but then she was summoned back to hell.

"What the-There's no way she can quickly go back that quickly," says Roman.

"It seems like she was summoned back. I think Satan or his grandkids summoned her back," says Sapphire. Roman flew up to the sky and spread lighting all over.

"Oh, crap!!" Says Xavier. The warriors flew down, and the demons got struck really hard.

"Oh my God, that lighting. That full power," says Sonny. They spotted Roman. He smiled at them.

"Roman..." says Tristan. The demons vanished.

"Huh? Are they gone? Forever?" asked Elizabeth.

"No, it looks like they been summoned back," says Sashell. The power vanished from Roman, and he flew back.

"Guys. I met him..." "Who? Wait, you don't mean...?"

"Yes. I met Jesus Christ."

"Amazing."

"At least no demons attack any people's heart." Says Sapphire arriving with Julmarie.

"I'm sorry, guys, if only I didn't train, and people saw and you guys."

"It's okay because without that, you wouldn't meet Jesus," says Selena.

"That's true, and at least nobody almost lost a life," says Julmarie.

"Let's go home, we'll summon Ida tomorrow, plus it's getting late," says Cory.

"Late? Oh no! We got to go home." says Sonny.

"Why such a panic?" asked Winston.

"Eric." "Ugh, not that guy," says Sashell. "

He is our stepdad." says Abigail.

"Well, we should be getting, see you guys," says Josh. In hell, Satan arrived where the demons lounge.

"Your dumbasses, if only I gave the power to Jade, we would've got Sapphire!! Damn you ALL!!!" He attacked them. I don't know why I saved you; I could've just let Roman killed you!! Ugh! Fucking attacking them from above. Fucking Idiots!" He left. Satan Jr. arrived at Fire's Cell.

"Hey, baby."

"Ugh, I already told you not to call me that. You and I are not a couple!"

"Back in 1996, we were."

"Not really, I was under the control of your damn granddad and was imminently took to earth."

"Yeah, to fight her."

"Ugh, do you have someone else to annoy?"

"Nope, you're my only one. You do realize we nearly capture Sapphire."

"But you didn't. Just go away. I want to be alone." He entered and grabbed her cheeks.

"Hey!" "You're so pretty!"

"Ugh." She started to blush. On earth, the warriors reached home in Tristan room.

"Good, we made it on- [SNIFF]. That smell. It smells good." says Usher. They reached downstairs and saw that their mothers are cooking.

"Hey kids, I'm making meatloaf. Their eyes shine. "And it's ready."

"Thanks, mom." They sat around the dinner table. "So, how's your day?"

"It was fine. Thank you," says E.J.

"Yeah, real nice," says Roman.

Eleven

SCIENCE CENTER

It was morning. "AH! so good. It's 10:00 in the morning." Says Sapphire waking up. She got washed up, and it was already noon. The warriors arrived at the house.

"Hey, guys. What should we do next? It's Saturday." says Cory.

"How about we go somewhere?" asked Usher.

"Hello, guys. How about you all go to the Science Center. I heard they have something interest there you might love." says Serita appearing from the upstairs door.

"The Science Center? Mom, I haven't been there since 4th grade," says Sashell.

"But if we go there, nostalgia will hit you right in the face! I always loved the science fair," says Sapphire.

"Maybe we should go there; there's something over there we need." Whisper Sheldon.

"Yeah, you're right," Sheldon whispered back Shquana.

"Okay, mom, we'll go, but mom, downtown Hartford is far from here," says Britannia.

"Take the bus. It's only $1.75. Plus, it said the tickets are free at the place. Have fun," she says as she walked back inside.

They walked to the bus stop. "The Science Center? I have never been here for all the time we spent here," says Sonny.

"We don't even have that in Jamaica," says Monica.

"You're going to love it, so much cool things to explore. OMG, I had the best times there, and I can't believe the tickets are free," says Sapphire. "Sapphire, if you love the science center so badly, why didn't you go all this time before you realized you were a warrior?" asked Julmarie.

"I didn't have time, plus nostalgia is so going to hit me."

"I have a feeling the science center is going to give us a clue about our pass," says Cory.

"And what makes sure you think that?" asked his older sister Selena.

"Doesn't the science center have a hell of stuff? Our powers recommend planets. Sapphire, don't they have a spare room?" asked Cory.

"Oh, yeah. They do. I wish we were already there instead of taking the bus." Then they were already at the science.

"Huh? How did we get here already? Sapphire, what did you do?" asked Trishawna.

"I didn't do anything?"

"You said you wish. I think you used one of your powers."

"Wish? I can wish for stuff?"

"Well, who cares? We shouldn't disgust about things like that, especially at Downtown. Come on," says Serena. They walked in, and it was huge.

"Oh my God, this place is huge."

"Hello, may I help you? Are you all together?

"Yes!" says E.J.

"Well, you're all lucky. It's all free today."

"Thank you." They all started to explore.

"Whoa look at this stuff," says Usher, amazed. In hell, Satan was watching them through his crystal orb.

"Hmm, the Science Center The perfect place to attack. Plus, once they reached the space room, they'll be in huge problems after what they're going to see, and it'll be the perfect time to strike. DEMONS!!!" They arrived.

"You summoned our Lord."

"Today is going to be different. Spy on the warriors, they're at the Science Center. Don't attack until after they're out of the space room. They'll be in huge shocked once they see something they're going to ask. Now go, and don't screw up like last time."

"Yes, our Lord." They vanished. At the science center, Sapphire stopped at the space dorm.

"Hey, you okay, Sapphire?' asked Julmarie, walking up.

"Y-Yeah. This is the room Cory was explaining about." Then everyone arrived.

"Alright, just take a look at this part of the Science Center," says Sashell.

They all walked in. This isn't so bad. The place is dark, but it isn't so bad," says Re-Re. "Here's my planet," says Cory.

"SHH!" says Selena.

"Other people are here too," says Josh.

"So, is there a planet with seven elements?" whispered Sonny.

"I doubt that."

"Here's mines," says Serena and Selena.

Each went to their planet. Their powers are from. "Here's the sun. I wonder, why are my powers from this gas giant?" Then all the marry warriors and Guardians had a shocking wave.

ALL: "AH!" "What's wrong?" asked Tristan.

They all started to faint. "HEY!" The Jesus warriors picked them up, but then they started to have flashbacks about their kingdoms.

"What the hell? Tristan! Roman! What is this? Who is that man in some light above?" Asked Abigail.

"You see it? AH!, says Roman. The Marry Warriors and Guardians were in a dark room."

"Where are we? Space?" Then they saw a woman from each planet and the sun.

"Huh? Who are you?" asked Cory. They held out their hands.

"What the-Who are you?" But then they woke up. "We need to get out of here. This part of the center is giving us a hell of flash backs," says Abigail.

"How the hell do you guys have a flashback?"

"Geez, I don't know. Probably cause of you guys," says Gabriella.

"Wait we need to stay a little longer. This could give us a clue," says Cory.

"You can say this hurts," says Serena.

"No! He's right. Who are those women?" asked Britannia.

"Woman?" says the Jesus Warriors.

"You don't see a woman?" asked Josh.

"No, all we see is an element kingdom the resembles our powers." Explain Abigail. "The guardians and Marry warriors close their eyes tight, and they resumed seeing the woman still holding out their hand."

"Who are you?" asked Josh. "I don't think we should trust them, what if they're from Satan."

"Didn't Tristan explain Jesus had a white glow all over his body?" asked Britannia.

"That is true," says Sashell. They each grabbed the woman who was on their planet and they each were glowing and then felt a little pain. They woke up and ran out of the space dorm.

"Let's get out of here," says Abigail. They ran out. But then Demons were above them and hit them with an attack, and it was an explosion.

Twelve

FIGHT AT THE CENTER

Whn the explosion done accrued, there was a force field protecting them from the attack by The God Warriors. "You guys are you okay?" asked Junior.

"God Warriors," says Josh in excitement.

"The cost is clear; transform," says Roderick. They transformed, but still had headache injury.

"What's wrong?" asked Trishawna.

Then the demons attack, but the God warriors used a shield. Both Roderick and Allyson flew up and attacked them with beams, but they dodged.

"It's just the fact that when we stepped in the space room, we started to have a headache, and us guardians and Marry Warriors met a woman in space in each planet," explained Cory.

"Us Jesus warriors started to have a vision about some elements kingdom being attacked as well," says Gabriella. "Then you guys should rest and protect Sapphire; we'll take care of them." "No, we're fine. Let's take care of them," says Sashell. Sashell flew up towards Zack, and he flew towards her. They collided each other fist and started to do combat towards each other and started to clash through the center top. The other warriors started to attack the other demons. Over where Sashell and Zack were they both back up.

"So, I see, you met someone, huh?" he asked.

"That's none of your concern!" he dodged and vanished.

"What?" He appeared behind her and dropped kick her to the floor.

"Ugh!" "Oh, come on Guardian of the planet Venus, you weren't that weak before."

"I've always beaten you Zack. Don't mess with me!" She charged at him full speed and kicked him down.

"What the hell?" "Who was that? I never got that speed before..." she whispered.

"Hmph." "Alright, you're so going to pay!" He charged at her at the Marry Warriors' side. Both Julmarie and Winston blasted beams at Lois and Aleg, but they dodged and was above them.

"I got you!" yelled Lois. They blasted beams at them, but they used a shield.

"What about that was a direct hit!" says Aleg.

But then Julmarie was behind them, and he hit them with a powerful sphere they crashed out of the center.

"Whoa. That power."

"We must've got it from those women we saw," says Winston.

"True."

Then another part of demons been blast off to the grown." "Whoa." It was from the rest of the Marry warriors.

"Damn! This is so cool," says Cory. Jade was flying down and attack the woman who was at the register.

"Let's see if you have the lying sin!" She looked, and there was no black dot.

"Aww damn... It looks like it's time to kill you."

Then a bright yellow attack came and it hit her. "Oh no, you don't!" yelled Sapphire flying down with Britannia.

"Ugh! Well, I should bring you down to hell with me."

"Like that's ever going to happen!" Britannia attacked her with blue beams, but she dodged.

"Damn it!" She appears above and blasts dark beams at them, but Sapphire used a shield.

"Sapphire, I'll take care of her. You go on and take care of the victim." She nodded and ran towards the victim to heal her. Jade kept attacking, but then spotted Sapphire running to the victim.

"Oh no, you don't." "CHA!" Yelled Britannia with a powerful beam. "Ah!" She crashed to the ceiling, and Britannia followed.

They on at the ceiling. Jade quickly got up and created a huge dark orb and blasted it at her but, she used a shield. It was pushing her back, but then she quickly moved out the way. Britannia flew up and started to realized beams at her, but she was dodging. In the center. Sashell flew back.

"You can't win, Sashell. I always wanted to do this." He turned completely black.

"What the-" He vanished and was instantly behind her and kicked her.

"Since when did he-" She turned around trying to punch him, but he was behind her and kicked her down. "HAHAHA. This is the power that Lucifer Jr. lends me. He instantly vanished and kept hitting her at every angle. She screamed in pain as she was getting the hits. As soon as he was going to hit again, she smirked and quickly snapped her fingers.

"Huh? What the-" he was paralyzed.

"Why am I paralyzed? How did you?"

"You're forgetting Venus is basically the sun, but a planet, and you're not the only one who has new powers, as you were hitting me, I secretly implanted something inside of you, some dust."

"Son of a-" "This ends now!" She spins and dropped kick him to the ground. Then on the ceiling, Jade crashed to the ground while an injured Britannia float down. Sapphire started to heal the victim. Then a miracle happened.

"Huh? What is this?"

A huge yellow aura floated the room, and it injured all the demons who were battling against the other warriors. They were hurt badly and crashed down where Zack and Jade are.

"Huh? What Happened?" Asked the victim. Sapphire started to fly up and see the demons have been beaten.

"What was that, aura?"

"I think it came from Sapphire.

"Not Just me. I think it came from the woman we saw in the space room." The demons vanished.

"Crap! They escaped. No worries, we already beat them, and it looks like no one has the Lying Sin here."

"True, we should head back home," says Cory. They all flew up and headed back to each of their houses.

Thirteen

THE ECLIPSE

I n Hell, Satan was twitching his eyes. "Let me guess, are you going to yell at the demons?" asked Satan Jr. as he arrived.

"Damn it! Damn it all! Those sons of bitches, Queens of the planets, and dwarfs appeared and helped them power-up, including Kaguya. I know those moves anywhere! It's them!"

"But what about the Jesus warriors?" "Remember the Jesus warriors control the seven elements. They're connected to the Guardians and Marry Warriors, hell even the Joseph Warriors. I haven't seen them yet," says Lucifer Jr. arriving. "And we also didn't see the rest of the guardians. My demons would've defeated them with strategy since Kaguya and the queens want to play that game. Let's give it to them! Demons!' They arrived.

"Yes, my lord?" asked Lucy.

"You're going to get a new power. From someone, to boost your power, and it's certainly not my grandchildren or me, but her. Satan Jr.?" He nodded and vanished.

In Fire's cell, Fire was meditating, but then Satan Jr. arrived.

"Listen, boy, I'-" He then attacked her taking away some aura from her; she screamed in pain and got knocked out. He then vanished and appeared back in the office.

"Here it is, you have some of Fire's powers aura. Use it now to destroy those warriors and capture, Sapphire. He sprinkled the aura around them, and they powered up. They were all amazed by this power.

"Thank you! Now then, let's go." They vanished. 6-minutes before, Sapphire, Britannia, Ally, Elizabeth, and Monica returned home from the science center and quickly de-transformed.

"Hey? How come Aunty Serita wanted us to go to the science center so bad?" asked Ally. "Yeah, there was nothing surprising about it except on what happened in the space room," says Monica.

"Who knows? Coincidence?" asked Britannia.

"Well, we shouldn't care. It's still the middle of the day, why did we separate, we should invite them," says Elizabeth.

"Already here," says Tristan arriving with everyone.

"We should all go to the park," suggested Sheldon.

"No way, what if the demons attacked," says Shquana.
"They already know our identities," says Cory.

"Yeah, but what if we don't have time to transform, they'll attack us within a second." Then Sapphire collapse.

"Sapphire!' shouted Julmarie. He held her up; then she started to spit out blood.

"What's going on? What's happening to her?" asked Josh?

"Uh, guys...Look at the moon..."Says Britannia pointing up. They looked outside and noticed the moon is red.

"Why is the moon out? It's 3 p.m.," says Abigail.

"And it's red, like pitch red, the last eclipse wasn't that red," says Serena.

"I think this is a sign; something is going to happen," says Usher.

"We need to get prepared. Josh and I will take Sapphire to her room, you guys transform and look for the demons if they're attacking," says Tristan. They nodded. Their fairies appeared and transformed. Tristan and Josh tried to pick up Sapphire, but she was too hot.

"Ah! " yelled both of them. "What's wrong?" asked Re-Re.

"She's hot."

"I think it's her powers," says Rihanna.

"I got an idea, Tristan transform," says Winston. He transforms and lifts up Sapphire.

"It doesn't burn."

"Let me see," says Josh as he transformed. He tried to pick her up, but he got burned again.

"What the heck?"

"I think cause it's due to Tristan powers," explained Roderick.

"Fine I'll take her to her room, from the outside, someone has to open her window."

"I'll do it," suggested Roderick. He de-transformed and ran upstairs. Tristan Flew outside to her room, and everyone flew up in the sky.

"Now where are those demons?" asked Sashell. Inside Roderick continues to run upstairs and open her room window. Tristan places her on her bed.

"At least the bed isn't melting. I'll catch up." Tristan nodded and joined the others.

"Sapphire...I wonder why you're like this?" He held her hand, but he wasn't burned; he saw something.

"What's this? The future?" It shows a girl who looks exactly like Sapphire getting attacked by Satan Jr.; he gives it to the demons.

"Oh, my God... They have power from...Sapphire...? No, that's not Sapphire...That's a girl who looks like her...Oh, no..." He let go.

"Oh, my God. I just saw the future by touching her. She's a twin...? No... I saw the demons powered up. They have powers from her twin. I have to stay here. To protect her."

While the warriors were flying around, they spotted nothing. "Where are the demons?" asked Junior.

"I guess they're not on earth," says Allyson. Then a dark orb came flying down.

"Watch out!" says Sashell using a shield, but her shield got broke as soon as the orb hit. She crashed hard on the ground.

"Ah! What the heck? What energy!" The demons arrived. "What's this? They have a red aura?" asked Julmarie.

"Where is Sapphire?" asked Max.

"That's none of your business." Max then attacked Britannia from corners so fast and kicked her down to the ground towards her sister.

"What speed...," says Gabriella.

"Now then, where's Sapphire?" He asked again.

"We'll never tell you where she is," says E.J.

"Fine guess we'll beat the truth out of all of you, and just to make it fair." They duplicated themselves.

"What the-" says Roman. "Get ready." They charge with speed. The warriors were getting prepared. In Sapphire's room, Roderick then touched Sapphire again and closed his eyes. This time he was transformed into his warrior form and met Sapphire in a white room. "Sapphire?" "Roderick? Where are we?"

"I have no idea." "Nice to see you again, Sapphire, Roderick..." "W-Who are you...?" asked Sapphire. "Wait, I saw you, but you were knocked out by Satan Jr."
"God healed me quickly so I can message you and looks like Roderick too."

Fourteen

NEW ECLIPS POWER

The warriors were getting pretty beaten up. "Are you guys really going to take this ass, whooping?" asked Lois flying down with her double.

"If you can take the ass whooping, we received to you, I'm pretty sure we can as well," says Cory. "AH! You little!" says Aleg. They blasted mega beams, but they dodged but barley.

"Tell us where Sapphire is located."

"NEVER!" says Re-Re.

"Fine. Keep receiving this ass whooping," says Peter. In the house, inside Sapphire's dream, both Roderick and Sapphire was in shock.

"What do you mean, my triplet sister? Where's the other one?" asked Sapphire.

"I don't have time to explain; I'm only using some of my power to connect to you. Sapphire, Satan Jr. token away my some of my powers and gave it to the demons because of what happened in the science fair. The only way to boost the warrior's strength to theirs, if you go to the movie, and that's where Roderick kicks in."

"Why me?"

"You're the only God Warrior who seen flashbacks of your past because of Sapphire, and you have to protect her, take her to the sky and let her do the work. There the sun will ride and give the warriors boost, and they'll match the demons."

"Can't they just go to their powers? Like what happens in the science center?"

"That only happens once. Plus, The God Warriors don't have that power."

"Oh yeah, guess it's really up to you, Sapphire."

"Well, mostly you, I need to be protected, and we need to get to the sky, but what am I supposed to do?"

"You'll know. Oh, and before you go." She summoned a sleeping guinea pig.

"What the...A guinea pig?"

"You'll need him, he'll be very useful to the angel fairies." she handed her the mammal.

"Now, go!" She vanished, and both Sapphire and Roderick woke up. "Ah!" Then she looked outside and spotted no demons. "There are no demons in sight."

"But we still need a disgusted." Roderick pulls out some blankets and cuts some holes.

"There we can dress ourselves like Muslim women and find a faraway place so we can fly to the sky.

"Damn, if only we had invisibility, that be so much better."

"Wait, don't you have that wish ability?"

"Yeah...Uh. I wish me and Roderick were in the sun already." But nothing happened.

"I guess it's not working. Come on."

"Wait about the Guinea pig."

"[GASPED] Is that who I think it is?" says the sun fairy.

"It is!" says The God fairy.

"What?" asked Roderick, all confused.

"This is the guinea pig who heals us.

"Just leave him here," says The God Warrior fairy creating a cage for the sleeping guinea pig. Sapphire placed him in the cage, and they head to the door. They hear the battle noise from a distance away.

"Man, it seems like some tuff battle," says Roderick.

"All because of me. They're searching for me, and I forgot to ask fire why they're after me."

"We'll ask later; we're wasting time. Let's go." They say as they continue to walk disguised as Muslim women. The warriors got beaten down; most still were in the sky fighting.

"I really don't understand your warriors. Just give up. Just know that we won!" says Aleg.

"Come on, lighting power, where are you?" asked Roman. "Oh, and that power you, and Tristan had. They won't be coming back. You're all goners now!"

"Wait for Lois," says Lucy.

"We'll ask again, where is Sapphire?"

"What do you even want with her?" asked Josh.

"Her sun powers."

"Kind of yes, and she's the key, she needs to go with her sister."

"Sister?" thought Sashell in surprised. Then Zack hit him.

"Idiot, why the hell you tell the enemy our plan, great! Thanks to you, they'll never tell us where she is."

"Capture her? For what?"

"It's none of your concern!"

"You said it was for Satan's plan. No way!" says Serena.

"Looks like we got to destroy the whole neighborhood until we find her," says Lois.

They were all in shock. They instantly separated, and the warriors were in shocked then follow. Both Sapphire and Roderick were still running; then they hear explosions.

"What the-Are they really out of their minds?"

"Don't look back; we're not going that way. We still need to get to the woods," says Sapphire. They reached and uncovered themselves.

"Alright, right here is good. Come on, Angel fairies." They transformed and started to fly up. The demons continue to destroy stuff until Lucy spotted both Sapphire and Roderick flew above them.

"There she is!" She pointed, yelling.

"Crap!" says Roderick. They charged at them so fast, but then the warriors created a shield altogether.

"Ugh!" "Where are you going, Sapphire?"

"I need to go to the sun; Fire told me to."

"Sapphire, I'll stay here; continue your request to the sky." She nodded and flew up.

"Oh no, you don't, Sapphire!" Says Peter rushing in, but then the Jesus warriors, attack but he dodged quickly.

"Ugh, you all are such a pest!" Sapphire started to fly up, and the Jesus warriors followed. The demons were going to follow too put the God warriors stopped them. Both Sapphire and the Jesus warriors arrived.

"Here we are. It's kind of looked like heaven," says Gabriella. "No time. Sapphire, do your stuff."

"Uh...I really don't know what to do."

"Did fire really not tell you anything?" asked Usher.

"Sapphire the warriors are getting beaten up, what are you supposed to do?"

"I'm going to give you just as much speed and strength as the demons are having right now." "And how?" asked Sonny.

"Uh, guys look at Roman and Tristan," says Gabriella.

All: "Huh?" They all looked back and their eyes were as the same color as their powers. Tristan's was red, and Roman was white.

"Are they possessed or something?" asked Abigail, a little frightening.

Roman flew closer and tapped Gabriella in the shoulder and she too becomes one, but her eyes were the color baby blue.

"They're turning them into zombies!" says Usher.

"No, they're not," says Sapphire. Tristan then tapped E.J. and he became one and his eyes were dark blue. Gabriella touched Usher, and his eyes were orange. E.J. touched Sonny and his eyes turned brown, and lastly, Abigail got touched by Sonny and her eyes turned blue. Color of their eye's aura appeared and swirl around Sapphire, she begins to stare at the sun and notices a woman. Sapphire became numb, and the woman walked down and hugged her. Then a huge light from the sky dash out and everyone was stopped what they were doing, including the people in the city.

"What's going on?" asked Re-Re.

"This light?" says Allyson.

"It's so warm," says Rihanna. "Sapphire, you did it," says Roderick. Then each light started to hit each warrior and they were in an orb. "What the hell is going on?" asked Jade.

"THEY'RE POWERING UP!! ATTACK!" Yelled Zack. They all did an attacked together, but then the seven elements dash through the sky down and it destroys the attack. The Jesus warriors dashed down and had a yellow aura surrounding them.

"N-No way," says Lucy. Then each warrior had the same aura, then here comes Sapphire.

"Now! The battle getting real demons!" says Sapphire flying down.

Fifteen

XXXXX

The demons were a bit in shocked, but then they started to attack, but then they dodged instantly.

ALL: "WHAT?"

Each was behind them, but they used a shield. Then they all begin to fight in warp speed, clashing through all over the skies. People then started to be noticed and watched, then news reporters came and started to film. They stopped and dash at each other eyes, then look down.

"Oh great, we called in some paparazzi," says Winston. "We need to get these people away," says Sashell. "How? They can't understand us, nor see our full-body," says Trishawna. "Okay, looks like we got to ember vise" Sashell flew down trying to warn the people to get away, but Zack appeared from above and hit her with his powers. "AH!" She cried as she smashes to the ground. The people were in huge shocked, then Zack tries to attack them, but then all the God warriors created a barrier to protect the people who were about to get hit by the attack, then the other warriors charged down to fight them. The people started to run away.

"Alright shits about to get real, huh?" The demons have been summoned back.

"Huh? They're gone?" asked Rihanna.

"Who cares? Let's go home. I'm missing moms' dinner," says Roderick.

"And it's getting close tonight and the people are still staring, and great we're gonna be on the news," says Serena.

"Well, at least they won't know our identities," says Junior.

"I'm out." They all vanished except for Britannia, Sapphire, and Sashell. They flew down and started to heal Sashell.

"Sashell are you okay?" asked Britannia flying down with her sister.

"Yeah, I'm alright. I can believe I let my guard down towards that demon."

"It's okay. I'll heal you." Sapphire started to heal her, then paparazzi started to arrive and tried to take pictures, but the two quickly grabbed their older sister and flew off.

"I swear, paparazzi can be so annoying," says Britannia. "They just want some photos of the warriors that protecting them from the demons," says Sapphire. They arrived home and de-transformed, but Sashell was a little hurt.

"Ugh!" "How are you still hurt in your human form?"

"It's probably I got a direct hit from him, and I let my guard down." Their fairies arrived, and they flew upstairs.

"Hey, where did you think you guys are going, somebody can see you," says Britannia.

"I doubt that, since they can't see our physical bodies, or understand us, I doubt they're going to see the fairies," explain Sashell.

"Wait, I know where they're going," says Sapphire as she runs up the back steps. Monica opened her window and saw her cousin running up the steps.

"Hey, what's going on?"

"Our fairies," says Britannia holding her injured sister.

"She's still injured huh?" Then Monica fairy, plus her sisters, started to fly to Sapphire's back window.

"What's going on?" asked Ally, coming to the window to look up.

"Seems like they're going to Sapphire's room."

"Come on girls, Follow me. I know why." She continues to run up the steps and they were into the house and went to Sapphire's room, and what they saw was a guinea pig healing the fairies.

"What the- What is that?" asked Ally.

"That's a guinea pig," replied Elizabeth. "Not just any guinea pig. This is the guinea pig my sister Fire gave me."

"Sister? You have another sister?" asked Sashell.

"Yes. She says we're triplets, but I don't even know where the other one is... How is that possible."

"Relax, we'll meet her one day or save her. What's her name?"

"Fire." "Fire? The element fire what Tristan possessed?"

"Yes...That's her name. Roderick and I met her when I was passed out just a while ago, and she told me about what to do. She's the main reason you guys had a boost, and she gave me this guinea pig. It seems like the fairies are attached to him."

"Fairies, what can the guinea pig do?" asked Elizabeth.

"He can heal us." "So, God created him?"

"Technically speaking, no... Someone in the Zatterverse did. A genius, man."

"What?" Asked Britannia in shocked.

"A Zettaverse? What's that?" Asked Monica.

"It sounds like another universe, but it's not."

"A Zettaverse is not a universe; it's bigger than a universe, even a multiverse, even the Hyper verse." Explain Ally's fairy.

"Wait, how big is this Zettaverse?" Asked Sashell.

"Very big. Like she says bigger than a multiverse, a Hyper verse, a mega verse, almost the size of the omniverse, but a little small, plus space there is different on how you can tell. There the space color is white and blue." Explain Britannia's Fairy. They were all in shock.

"Who is this man's name in the Zettaverse?" Asked Elizabeth.

"His name is David." Both Sapphire and Britannia was in more shocked.

"Our father?" Asked Britannia.

"No, he just has the same name as your dad."

"How much.... verse is there in space?"

"Well there is a universe, then Multiverse, then Metaverse, then Xentaverse, Hyper verse, Mega verse, Kilo verse, Peta verse, Giga verse, Hectoverse, Traverse, ExtaVerse, Zettaverse, Yattoverse, then the omniverse, then this is not a verse, it's just a very powerful Godly thing called the Box, then there's the infinity, then out is Heaven and hell."

"Oh, my God. Then which verse are we in?" Asked Elizabeth.

"We're in the omniverse." Says Sashell Fairy. She came to Sashell and healed her all around, and she was completely fine.

"Ah! That's much better. If we're in the omniverse, does that mean we'll have the ability to go to an omniverse level?"

"Maybe, if you work hard to achieve it." Says the guinea pig. They were all shocked, including the fairies.

ALL: "You can talk?"

"Of course! I do have a human form, thanks to David." He Transform.

"Oh my gosh."

"Yup. David is a well-known good scientist. I'm not the only one, he has all the animals living in his tropical island with his 11 kids who have superpowers and wife, plus they have insects who have human forms, but some are not even on that earth, some are on different planets keeping it save from some evil scientist who wants to capture those powerful beings. Insects are the only ones who have a monster insect that has the same DNA. Plus, each planet has David siblings and nibbling's sealed protecting that planet from those evil scientists. Only six insects are on earth. Plus, they have vampires living with them too."

"He conducted vampires. How did he become a vampire?" Asked Sapphire.

"I don't know to ask him. I don't get near them."

"This David guy must be a real help."

"That can't happen?" "What do you mean?" Asked Elizabeth.

"David is the guardian of the Zettaverse and a spiritual one."

"Aww, crap. It looks like he's off the chart. We have to keep our eyes open tomorrow for what the demons are planning to attack next," says Ally.

"That's true. It's a pleasure to meet your guinea." He shook his head and fell asleep." "Girls! Dinner ready." "Time for food." the girl's dash downstairs.

Sixteen

USHER PART I

The Jesus warriors was just done eating. "Thank you for the meal, mother," says Gabriella. She nodded her head and took up the dishes, they were ready to go to bed, but they all went to Usher room.

"Man, what's going to happen tomorrow."

"We need to keep our eye up. The demons can attack no time."

"But what about those dreams. It seems like it hurts." Says Usher. "They don't; it just shows you where you're from. I wonder whose Jesus is going to choose to get that power," says Roman.

"Maybe me," says Abigail.

"No way. Me," says Gabriella.

"We just have to wait, but either way, we'll still get that power. We serve Jesus anyway. He'll choose," says Sonny.

"That's True. Well, it's getting late, those demons sure can pick up a fight, and they waste our entire Saturday," says E.J.

"We still have Sunday. I hope the demons don't attack us Sunday," says Sonny.

"True. [YAWN]. Well, good night guys," says Abigail as she was walking out. They all soon followed. Usher went on his bed, and his fairy arrived.

"Hey, fairy."

"Yes?"

"Do you know what's it's like to have that amazing power what my two older brothers have?"

"You had that power back then."

"What year?" "I think in the 1700s."

"Aww, man. That time. I thought the 1900s."

"And what makes that better?"

"We're in the 2000's I thought you'd remember."

"Oh...Uh...Right." "I can't waste time. Good night fairy."

"Good night usher." He vanished and Usher fell asleep. Time has flown by and Usher was turning and twisting in his sleep, then he was still dreaming, but he opens his eyes and saws a man right in front of him.

"Oh my! What the-Huh? Jesus." The man smiled and lent out something, and it placed in him.

"Huh?" "Follow me." Usher got up and followed him. In the real-world Usher was sleepwalking and his eyes were glowing baby blue, and he begins to walk out. His fairy was summoned by forced and he began to follow him. The angel fairy tries his best to stop, but his body wouldn't obey his orders, so he had to call the other angel fairies through the mind.

"Guys, Help! Help! There's something wrong with Usher."

"What is it, the fairy of air?"

"He's like sleepwalking. Warn the others. My body won't obey me, but my mind would. Just warn the others to stop him." The other angel fairies appeared of each of the Jesus warrior's bedroom and tried to wake them up.

"Get up! Get up!" Says The earth angel fairy.

"Hmm...Go away." Mumbled Sonny.

"It's your brother. Usher. He's in trouble."

"What...?" He was woken up. Each sibling opened their door and saw usher walking down the steps.

"Come on." Whispered Gabriella. They followed Usher. He entered the woods. "The woods...? I'm scared of the woods, especially at night," says Gabriella.

"You're a Jesus Warrior. I'm surprised you're not scared of heights. Let's go," says Sonny.

They walked into the woods and saw a big no tree's field and Usher was in the middle. His Angel fairy went in him, but he didn't transform.

"What's going on?" Usher begins to glow bright, and a twister begins to appear.

"OH CRAP!" Yelled Roman.

"Transform quick!" Yelled Tristan.

They quickly transform with a dash of light and fly away from the twister.

"What is up with him? USHER!" Shouted E.J. Usher fell down.

They were all a little shocked. The twister disappeared and half the woods were destroyed. "Thank goodness the fairies were here, and we transform just in time," says Roman. Then there was a car crash.

"Huh?"

Then some people who were on the streets were passing out.

"What's going on?" "Why is everyone passing out?" Then Usher stood up and another twister appears much bigger.

"Oh no, you don't!" Says E.J. He froze the twister, but it cracks the ice and it still approaches, then it got bigger and bigger.

"Oh, crap." "Damn looks like I pissed him more off," says E.J. But then the twister vanished, and usher fainted.

"Hey, I don't sense any powers in him," says Tristan.

"Wait." E.J. created an ice shield over him.

"Seriously?" asked Abigail.

"Either that or another twister." They flew down and grabbed usher. "Usher? Usher?" He was completely passed out.

"Oh my gosh, he's passed out. What should we do?" "Well, we can't stay here. Somebody will see or spy on us. Let's go to the sky." And what if he did another twister, it'll be much worse, and it's from the sky," says Tristan.

"I doubt it. I have his angel fairy, but he's badly injured. What shall we do?" Asked Roman. "Let's fly up." They started to fly out of the ice shield.

"Wait. Sonny grabbed the ground where the ice shield is on." He nodded and controlled the grass ground and brought it up, and they flew up to the sky. They went above the clouds and landed on the grass ground float that E.J. was controlling.

"We'll be safe here."

"But those people I wonder why they were passing out," Sonny questioned. Satan was watching them from his orb.

"Oh my. It looks like the Jesus warriors are in trouble for what the air one did. This will be a great opportunity to find the evil sin and kill Jesus warriors once and for all. I wonder why Jesus let his air one did that, and he's the strongest one out of all the Jesus Warriors." He snapped his fingers. On earth, the Jesus Warriors were looking around, seeing people passed out.

"Hey, guys, could this be they're not getting enough air?" Asked Roman.

"That could be it...But we got to look out for the demons," says Tristan.

"Look out!" Pointed and shouted Abigail. A dark cloud beam was coming to them. E.J used harden ice shields to protect them, and it was the demons.

"Aww, great, now demons."

"Look down too," says Gabriella.

"They're attacking some people. Damn you demons!" Tristan tracked them down, but the demons arrived and used a shield.

"Ugh!" "Games over Jesus warriors, you're too busy protecting your brother!" Says Zack. They attack, but then the God warriors appeared and used a shield.

"You guys, okay?"

"Yeah." E.J. summoned mud all over the world, and it hit some demons. "Why didn't you do that earlier?" Asked Lucy.

"Can't you see I'm controlling something else. I had to drop this in order to do the other, as a matter of fact." He summoned back the ground object that they were on and threw it at the demons, but they dodged.

"Trishawna used sticky water and trapped her body, but she can still fly and the same goes for the other demons. Then Allyson used boon rainbow eggs, and they got hit. 'Damn that was a good collaboration," says Max.

In the bottom, Jade was attacking every person and seem like none of them had the lying sin. "Ugh no. Lying Sin. Time to die, all of you. Then a sun rod stung her. "Ugh! She looked up and saw Sapphire with the marry warriors and guardians.

"Alright. We'll take care of her. Sapphire go heal those people," says Josh. She nodded her head.

"I'll come with you, Sapphire," says Julmarie. In the sky, Tristan was holding onto his brother and flew down.

"Don't worry usher. I'll keep you save." In his mind, Usher was in front of Jesus.

"So that's why you did this so I can feel that power, but the people..."

"You'll achieve a brand-new power. Air is the strongest one out of the elements. Use it and see a new power you'll have and soon, your siblings will obtain that power as well, including the first two." He nodded and started to close his eyes, out in the real-world usher woken up still had baby blue eyes. He absorbed his angel fairy in him and transformed. Tristan quickly let go and backed up.

"What the-" Then everyone stopped and noticed. "What the hell... Another transformation?" Says Peter. "And from another Jesus warrior?" Usher was full of air wind aura.

"What the-Oh my." "Another brief transformation." Says Junior.

Seventeen

USHER PART II

A ir...!" He said in a lower tone voice. Air started to warp and attacked everyone. Earth started to rotate fast.

"Oh God, the planet!" Says Cory.

"He has the ability to control the planet?" Asked Sheldon in shocked.

"The people!" Shouted Serena. "Usher, stop!" Yelled Selena. Usher continues to control the wind, and it hit the demons hard with their clones.

"Ugh! What the hell. Since when the hell did, he gets this-No way!" Says Peter clone.

"Crap, it looks like he has that power as well with the other two Jesus warriors," says Jade.

"Who cares! We have some powers as well. Let's use Fire's power," says Aleg. They glowed red, and they render through Usher's air power.

"Guys, let's use our powers!" says Julmarie. They glowed yellow alongside Sapphire and charged at them. The Jesus warriors and Sapphire started to protect Usher.

"Usher, you need to control your powers. The people on this planet-"

"No need, Tristan. They'll come back."

"Come back? What?"

"Sapphire, come here." Sapphire flew down.

"What is it?" "Grab a hold on me." She went behind and grabbed hold onto her cousin. They both glowed yellow and a powerful wind arrow came towards the demons. The warriors noticed and jumped up.

"Jesus warriors use your powers towards my air power." "Water!" says Abigail.

"Fire!" Says Tristan.

"Earth!" Says Sonny.

"Lightning!" Says Roman.

"Ice!" Says E.J. "Frost!" Says Gabriella.

"Sun power!" It attached to the air arrow and collided. "Let's help them out," says Sashell.

"Marry Warriors attack!" Says all the marry warriors.

"God warriors attack!" Says all the God warriors.

"Mercury power!" Says Britannia.

"Venus Power!" says Sashell. It also attached to the arrow, and it came towards the demons.

"Let's dodged this," says Peter. "Oh no, you don't!" says Sapphire. It went to every angle surrounding their surroundings.

"Crap." They glowed redder and more tried to protect. It hit them, and they were struggling.

"Ugh, this power. They have us cornered and we're fucked." says Peter!" "Guess we got to return. RETURN!" They disappeared, and the attack disappeared.

"Darn, they got away," says Josh.

"Only because they were using Fire's powers," says Winston. The earth stops spinning fast, and the people were already dead.

"I don't see a living person alive," says Monica.

"Of course. The earth was spinning way too fast; it killed the people. What are we going to do about this?" asked Elizabeth.

"No need," says Usher flying down.

"Huh?" He landed. "Revival!" He glowed, and it reached all over the earth. Everyone was alive.

"What did he do?" asked Roderick. "I think he used the ability revival. He can bring back the dead," says Junior.

They all flew down. "Usher..." "No need. The rest of the Jesus warriors can do that too. Jesus explains it to me that I will learn a new ability. Revival. We shouldn't be here. God warriors erase their minds." They nodded and flew up erasing the people's minds believing they were dead. The warriors disappeared. In hell, the demons arrived back to their room.

"Damn, if it weren't for Fire's power, we'll be dead," says Max. "They had Sapphire for a little boost. If only we had Fire under the control of Satan, we'd stand a chance," says Zack.

"But we all know what happen last time; we nearly lost her. We just have to sit and wait until we capture Sapphire. Ugh!"

"Well, well, that was an unexpected power up," says Lucifer Jr. walking in.

"My lord. We tried; it seems like the strongest Jesus warrior achieves the same form."

"Man, if only we just had the lying sin already. "I'll be on earth and dispose of those warriors and take Sapphire, but that Jesus warrior could be very useful under my grandfather's power. He also has the ability to revival."

"But my lord, I thought all the Jesus warriors had that ability."

"Oh yeah, I totally forgot. We should probably keep a close eye on those warriors; they're getting more powerful. They weren't like this back in the previous centuries. Could this be Jesus doing...? No... I'll talk to my father. You guys get some rest and train. They lying sin is still out there.

" He walked out. In Satan's, office Satan Jr. was talking with his grandfather.

"Just look at that. He strongest Jesus warrior out there. He even controls the planet, who knows, soon he'll be at least omniverse or something due to him being Jesus warrior. His power was even stronger than the first two, and they're older than he is."

"It's no use. I pay close attention and they had Sapphire; it looks like he's not the only one who learns an ability. Sapphire can read minds and hear from far ahead. She controls the air using her sun powers and nearly killed the demons by every angle they were in, kind of like they were in a tornado. Sapphire is already proven to be stronger than all of them. We need just her, and only her." Says Lucifer Jr. arriving.

"If only we had the lying sin to be there already."

"Well, you two just got to sit and wait. We got to wait until we see who has the lying sin."

Eighteen

ABIGAIL PART I

The Jesus Warriors arrived at their house and quickly de-transformed.

"Well, we got to get inside; it's already sunrise. Damn. What time is it?" It's at 8 o'clock. Let's have a cookout with just us."

"Why not invite everyone?"

"Hmm...I don't know. Fairies contact them," says Tristan. They started to contact the fairies.

"Well, the rest of the warriors aren't really doing anything. So, you can throw a little cookout, but I can tell your parents are asleep," says Fairy of Fire.

159

"I really don't know what to do for now?"

"Well, we can go to the science center to get more answers."

"No! That was painful in the space," says Gabriella.

"Well, we won't go to the space room. Let's go to some other rooms," says E.J.

"The thing is E.J. we don't have any money, and it's not free tickets. Plus, it's a Sunday. They're closed," says Roman.

"Aww, man." "Do you guys want to go for a fly??" Asked Usher.

"Well, we got nothing else to do. We can just roam around through Downtown Hartford. Until time goes by, and we'll hand out with the rest of the warriors, and besides. If the demons attack, we'll probably be the first ones to beat them down," says E.J.

"That's true, but-" "But what?"

"What if-Actually I have another great idea."

"That is?" Asked Sonny. "We go to the mall." "No way!" "Please?" Begging Gabriella.

"No, and besides, that's what you two want because you're girls. Let's have a good sibling time and fly around the city. You fairies ready?" They nodded. They look around their surroundings to make sure no one is watching.

"Alright, it's clear. Let's go." They transformed and started to fly away.

"Wow, even the weather is better and it's close to falling."

"Well, it's a little bit of summer. It's the beginning of September already. We'll be fine." They roam around.

"Hey, guys, hungry?" Asked sonny.

"Yeah." They all said. Sonny controlled the tree branches and created some apples as they have grown all the way to the top.

"Aww! Thank you!" says Gabriella.

"And they're ripe," says Usher. They started to eat and started to fly; then they flew to the city.

"Whoa. I have never been to the city in Jesus' form. This looks beautiful from up here," says Gabriella.

"Hello? We always battle in the streets and forests. Never the city."

"I don't get it, Downtown Hartford has lots of people, why won't the demons attack here?" asked Abigail.

"Don't give them ideas! Who knows, Satan could be watching, and those demons could be anywhere in disguised," says Abigail.

"Oh yeah, disguised as what? In the air." "I don't know a skydiver," says Roman.

"Who cares about that. Let's go skate at the Hartford riverfront," says E.J. Pointing to the river. They flew to the river, and E.J. freezes it.

"Careful, don't hit the bridge." "I think I know how to control my powers, Sonny.

"They landed on the ice and began to skate. "I don't think I can skate well." Says Gabriella.

"You're the guardian of frost. How can you not know how to skate?" asked Abigail.

"Here, I'll teach you little sis," says Tristan. He begins to teach her, and the rest started to skate. Then out of nowhere, a giant water hand popped out of the ice. On the road bridge, there was a crash cause of the shocking of the hand.

"Abigail, what the hell?!" Yelled Roman.

"That's not me!"

Both Sonny and Usher flew to the bridge. "Sonny, just to let you know, Revival is only for humans and monsters not demons, fallen angels, or angels."

"How come, because Jesus told me. We're not at that level to revive those three. Let's just revive those people who got killed, if they did, and get out of here. It's already 12 0'clock. Damn, time is going so fast," says Usher.

"Abigail. Put it down."

'I'm trying." She put down the giant water hand back. Then another approach and it was coming towards her, then another crashed. E.J. freezes the hand solid.

"Abigail, this better not be a damn joke."

"I'm telling you, it's not me!!!" The people stopped and got out of their car and watch the action. Sonny and Usher arrived at the bridge.

"Revival," says Usher. The people who were in the car crashed been brought back to life.

"Earth!" He controls the branches to cover the bridge.

"Alright. That'll protect them. What is going on? What is up with the water." Then the ice started to melt, and the Jesus warriors flew away. The water began to go up once again to capture Abigail.

"ICE!" Yelled E.J. He freezes the water. Then some water went up to the sky and it got vaporized. The sky begins to have more clouds and it begins to rain. The water started to form, and hand connecting to the river and reached out to Abigail. She tries to control it, but it was fighting back.

"Ugh. It's like someone else is controlling the water, and they're much stronger than I am." She says as she struggled.

"Blue Fire!" He shoots out into the water, and it turned into steam.

"Nice job Tristan, not there's gonna be mist everywhere!" says Sonny. "Crap!" Then it begins to rain more.

"Ice!!!" Yelled E.J. He shoots it in the air, and it begin to rain hail. "E.J. What the hell!" says Abigail.

Usher turned around, but there was mist everywhere he couldn't really see. "Damn. Tristan light Fire so bright, it will clear the mist!!" Shouted Usher.

"Oh yeah!" Tristan glowed bright and expanded fire. The steam disappeared, and so did the clouds.

"Nice one," says Gabriella. Then the water did a sneak attack and grabbed Abigail, and quickly grabbed her to the water. "Abigail!" Yelled Sonny.

"I knew this was a bad idea. We should've gone to the mall." Complain, Gabriella. She was in the ocean.

"Damn, we can't survive in the water for too long. "Uh, yes, we can, we're warriors," says Roman.

"No, I meant. I meant we couldn't really see. This is dirty water," says Usher.

"Oh." Abigail opened her eyes, and it was like she was in some water. "What is this? Where am I?"

"Finally, it's nice to meet you..." says a woman. "Huh?"

It was the woman she saw in her vision at the Science Center. "Abigail..."

Nineteen

ABIGAIL PART II

You...You're the woman I saw in my vision at the center...How...?"

"I used my powers in order to meet you."

"I thought... Those were the demons, and we got scared. I'm-"

"It's alright the time has come for you to use your powers." 'Wait, the same as my three older brothers. Are we truly real brothers."

"Yes, even in the past, you're still half-siblings."

"[GASPED]. W-What do should we do in order to achieve this form."

"You must first control the planet's water all at once."
"What? I can already do that." "Not at once at the same time. You even struggled against me if you don't understand. They say you're in space and you need to lift all of earth's ocean up, all at once — not one by one. You used to do this in the past, but now you been reborn; it's going to be a little hard. Try to control the Pacific Ocean. Since it's the biggest ocean." They teleported to the Pacific Ocean.

"Whoa! Look at this. It's so beautiful."

"Yes, it is. Now control it. Try making a giant tsunami starting down here. It'll travel upwards. I'll create a simulation on what's going upwards. Go on.

"She nodded and started to control it, but it was a little too hard. Then in Hartford, the other Jesus warriors heard screams.

"Huh?" Then they saw the demons attacking some people at the same time.

"Crap, none of these people have the lying sin, and we're in the city," says Glenn.

"Well, we attacked six. There are lots more," says Jade. Then lighting came, and they dodged.

"You guys are such an annoyance," says Tristan flying with his siblings.

"Ugh, the warriors."

"Only the Jesus warriors. Hmm?"

"What's up?"

"There's six of them. Normally there's seven. Where's the seven one. That must mean she's getting a power-up!" Yelled Zack. They flew up. "ICE!" He blasted everywhere, but they teleported.

"What the-" They teleported to the river and attacked the ocean.

"That's odd. Normally she'll appear," says Max. Then another attack approach, but they dodged. The rest of the warriors appeared.

"That was fast."

"Careful, they can teleport."

"Since when they can teleport."

"Remember they have of Fire's power," says Josh.

"No, remember they can teleport back to hell. It looks like they upgrade it. This is gonna be tuff," says Julmarie.

"Remember, we can keep up with their speed. Where are the people who got attacked, let me hear them."

"Follow me," says Roman." She flew off with him. The demons watch Sapphire as she flew away with Roman.

"Oh no, you don't!" Then an energy blast hit Jade.

"Ugh, you guys are such an annoyance." "And you act like you're not either," says Sashell.

"Don't get cocky!" says Zack heading towards her. The rest of the demons duplicated themselves and headed for the warriors. Sapphire reached the people who were attacked.

"Wait, don't you have revival Roman?" Asked Julmarie.
"Yes, but they're not dead." Sapphire flew down and started to heal them. "We need to hurry up before-"

"AH!" Yelled Roderick as he crashed to a building.

"-Come to the city, and the people will crow the people I'm healing," says Sapphire finishing her sentence. Roderick stood up, and Peter clone was coming after him."

"Man, the battlefield is coming towards the city," says Julmarie.

"There I'm done. Let's get [GASPED]."

"Where do you think you're going, Sapph-AH!" Yelled Zack.

"We're not done," says Sashell.

"Sapphire come with us," says Roman. They flew up. "It's me they're after. We need to leave them out of the city. HEY! I'M RIGHT OVER HERE! COME AND GET ME!!"

"Sapphire, what the hell!" "It's the only way. We can't risk getting the city destroyed," says Julmarie. The demons spotted and chased after her. The three went away. "Wait Abigail is gone. That means she'll get a power-up like you and the other two. We just got to lead them to the river," says Julmarie.

"That is a great idea. I wonder what she's doing?" At the Pacific Ocean, Abigail was controlling all the water, even connecting to the oceans all over the planet.

"Hmm. You control it so quickly. Congrats." "I am the God of water, hold up." She closed her eyes and connected to the Hartford River. She sees a big battlefield. "Looks like the demons arrived. It is true, you want me to become like my brothers, but Jesus-" "Wanted me to do this so you can become

like your brothers." "What is Jesus to you." "....[SIGH] Basically my creator."
"[GASPED]...What...?" "There's no time. The warriors need you." She nodded. I can communicate with sea animals, can't I?"

"Yes." "Oh. Okay. I'm off." She vanished through bubbles.

"Good luck." She says as she watches Abigail vanished.

"My daughter." Sapphire, Julmarie, and Roman reached to the river. The demons followed who were the real ones.

"Looks like we got the real demons."

"Yeah." Says Roman.

"So, you really brought us to the river. This will be an easy capture."

"I hope Abigail knows what she's doing," says Roman.

"Hell hand!" A giant red hand appeared. "[GASPED]." The warriors spotted it above the river.

"Oh, no!" Yelled Allyson.

"No, you all don't!" Says the clones.

"Ugh!" "Grab Sapphire, and let's get this over with." Command Glenn.

"It came towards her. Roman was about to use lighting and Julmarie was about to protect, but then a huge wave protects them.
"Huh?" Then five waterspouts appeared and two whirlpools. Abigail appeared in her newest forms, like her brothers.

"She has the form. Sweet!" Says Roman.

"Water!" She shouted. It started to rain. "Guys, protection!" says Julmarie. They used protection.

"Sapphire, Usher, I need your help!" Shouted Abigail.

"Right!" They flew up, and so did Roman.

"This may injure the people, but with your sun powers to keep them warm and your air powers to keep them from drowning, the people will survive. Also, I can sense the demons put something in the city, that the next time we arrived, they bomb us."

"Don't you need Tristan fire powers to do that?" Asked Sapphire.

"To be honest, they'll use Fire's powers to move faster under my water. With your Sun powers to keep the people warm from this cold water and you'll give us a second boost of your power."

"Oh, okay. I see this is why I didn't want them to go to the city."

"And that's why they attacked the people in the city; I can see the bomb clearly with my water drops. The demons started to attack Abigail, but she used the water to protect herself, then the warriors arrived.

"Oh no, you don't!" Allyson as she dashed bomb eggs towards them.

"Now! TSUNAMI!!!!" "What...." says Sapphire, a little shocked. A huge gigantic water tsunami appeared out of the river colliding it with the rain.

"What is she doing?!" asked Roderick.

"Is she planning to destroy the city as well? The people!"

"Relax guys; the people won't get hurt. There's a bomb in the city that the demons planted in. Sapphire's using her sun powers, so it won't injure the people, the same as Usher, and destroy the bomb, that's why they attack the city, so the next time we go there, they'll bomb us."

"Oh. We better dodged and go up the clouds," says Shquana.

They flew up to the clouds and began to watch. The demons still attacked, but the tsunami gulped them up, and it hit the city.

"Guys, go in." Only the Marry warriors went in. The Demons could hardly see, but they were in the city. "Huh? I'm surprised the people aren't killed." The people were in shocked that they were breathing underwater.

"Well, we don't need to fly, we can just float," says Peter.

"Look out!" The Marry Warriors were coming in. Sheldon and Winston blasted beams at them, but they dodged.

"Ugh, huh? Why only the Marry warriors." Abigail rushed in while the whole city was underwater. Sapphire and Usher were still using their powers to maintain it, so the people won't down. The Marry warriors surrounded them and blasted beams at them every corner, and they bumped into each other.

"Ugh! Fire aura!" They all yelled. Abigail quickly glowed yellow; Sapphire quickly released yellow aura in the water, and Abigail created a whirlpool, trapping them. "We got you where we need you!"

"Damn it; they're using Sapphire aura as a boost.

"There's nowhere to hide! Let's destroy them once and for all so they won't attack innocent people anymore," says Josh. Above the ocean, both Sapphire and Usher got hit pretty hard with an energy blast. They crashed hard, but they were above the ocean, due to the fact that it's covering up all of Hartford.

"What the heck? Huh?" In the underwater, the people started to drown. "Huh? What's going on?" Asked Re-Re.

"They're drowning, and I don't feel o see Sapphire yellow aura wave." cried out Cory.

"Oh, crap!" Abigail was struggling to keep the demons at bay.

"Damn, it's going to be hard."

"Don't worry, we got your back," says Ally.

"But the people!" Yelled Xavier as he pointed down.

"Damn it!" "I'll take a look upwards," says Monica. Sapphire and Usher looked up and was a little shocked. They felt a huge amount of power from this guy.

"What the-Who is this guy. He has an amount of power in him...." says Usher. "Let's get rid of this water." He tapped his foot into the water, and it vanished. "What the hell? Where all the water goes?" Asked Elizabeth. Then all the Marry warriors were in shocked, looking at this creature.

"Lord, Anti-Christ!" They all said, bowing down. "Anti-Christ?!" They all yelled. The rest of the warriors dashed down from the clouds quickly from Sapphire's aura.

"What the hell...What's going on? Why do I feel an amount of aura from him? What type of person would have this aura?" Asked Sashell.

"You demons are such nescience. Get back to hell, and I'll deal with you later."

"Yes, our Lord." They vanished.

"Now then, give me Sapphire."

"N-Now way."

"You guys stand no chance against me." Their bodies move, and they crashed down to Hartford river playground.

"What the- How...My body just moves on its own..." says Abigail.

"Did he just use Reality Warping or something...?" Asked Rihanna.

"I think he did." He landed instantly. "Now, give me Sapphire, or else, someone's gonna die." "Never!" Shouted Abigail.

"Water!" She shouted. "A huge water hand appeared behind him, but it instantly vanished.

"AH! Damn it!" Shouted Abigail. "Shock orb!" Yelled Roderick. He blasted at him, but it turns into dust.

"What..." "Give me, Sapphire!" But then all of a sudden, they vanished.

"Damn it Jesus." He said looking up. He disappeared. They arrived at Rihanna and Roderick's backyard.

"What the hell...Where? Roderick and Rihanna house...?" Asked Tristan.

"Who was that guy?" "He was so powerful," says Junior.
"They say the Anti-Christ." 'Anti-Christ. Let's talk to Ida about
this," says Trishawna. They walked to the garage.

"Ida? Ida?" Asked Shquana. She arrived. She looked depressed.

"Ida...We need to talk to you about-" "No need, Abigail, I saw the
battle. I'll tell who was that you saw."

Twenty

SONNY PART I

That was the Anti-Christ. 1." "1? There are others?" "Yes, 3. The Anti-Christ is a triplet. He is the son of Satan."

ALL: "WHAT?! I thought Satan Jr. and Lucifer Jr. were Satan's sons," says Sapphire.

"No, those are his grandchildren — basically, the first Anti-Christ's sons. The first Anti-Christ is the first one to come out; his other two are somewhere. He probably arrived because you guys were going to kill the demons once and for all."

"Oh, I see, man but the city." "No need, God already fixed it. He even erased the people's minds about what happened, also congrats Abigail now you can most likely control any liquid."

"Wait, not just water?" "Nope. Any liquid, even saliva." "Ew...But I nearly put thousands of lives at risk, just to get rid of a bomb."

"No need, you have revival." 'Oh....Uh...okay." "I nearly got captured...."

"But you didn't. Hey, it's still daytime, only just. 2 o'clock. Want to go somewhere?" Asked Junior.

"All together?" Asked Selena.

"That's great, but we don't have any money," says Monica.

"No need. Money." Money arrived from the little sphere Ida summoned. "What the-You can summon things." "Of course, and since heaven is filled with gold and gems and stuff, it can have money too. Here you all go. This is 1,000$. Have fun at the zoo." "Aww crap, my fairies, they're injured," says Sheldon.

"Oh yeah. Ida mind summoning Guinea pig?" "Of course." She summoned Guinea pig.

"Hello, Sapphire." "What the hell? A guinea pig can talk."

"I am not any ordinary guinea pig; this guinea pig was created by a scientist in some verse called Zettaverse." 'Zettaverse, what's that?" Asked Josh.

"Some verse that's bigger than a universe and a Multiverse." 'So, which verse we're in?" "The omniverse."

ALL: "WHAT?" "How is that even possible, we're in the verse that the creation of all existence?" Asked Tristan.

"Yes. And this guinea pig even has a human form." Says Ida. The guinea pig transforms into her human form. "Hello. I'll heal your angels." They float to him, and they instantly healed. "Wow, so much better it's a pleasure to meet you." Says fairy of the planet Make-Make. "We need to go to the Zoo. Ida, mind teleporting us there?"

"Of course." She teleports them directly inside the zoo." "Hey, look on the bright side at least we don't have to pay," says Cory.

"Yeah, but how are we going to get down from this tall tree?" Asked Selena. "No need," says Cory. He controls the ground creating steps. "Thanks, Sonny," says Re-Re. "No problem." They walked down. "Hurry, before someone sees us," says Sashell.

They walked down fast. As soon as they walked down, they been spotted by some people. "Hey! How did you get down here? Actually, where did these steps come from?" "A new thing the zoo has. One step up there, you can see the whole park." Explain Serena.

"Oh. Come on son, let's go. "Alright, we're at the zoo. What are we supposed to do?"

"Let's have fun remember, we waste half our day fighting the demons and nearly got whipped out by the Anti-Christ guy. Let's enjoy our day, and hopefully lookout if the demon's attacks." Says Ally.

"Um...Okay." They begin to walk around. In hell, Satan was watching them through his orb. "Fuck. If only that bitch Abigail didn't see the bomb I implanted, well luckily, my son put them in their place." "You know what's funny, how could the father be on earth, but not me or my brother?"

"Isn't obvious, he has more of grandpa blood than we do, we have less, and they have a limit time on earth, they have more powers than we do, and for the guard, Jesus sealed all off in here for a good 20 years until the time is right until they went to the age when they first fight us back in1414." Explain Satan Jr.

"Now we got to find this lying Sin, so we won't have limit time to be on earth to get Sapphire. Ugh. What the hell is going on, why didn't Father just use reality warping to get Sapphire and bring her to hell?"

"Isn't it obvious? Jesus summoned them back and he ran out of time," explain Satan. "They're at the Zoo." "Good so many hostages."

"They do have the power to revive people." "

They're not that evil, look on what happened with Abigail." " have an idea."

"What is it?" "How about we attack the earth's core?" "Wouldn't that kill all life on earth except them?" "And we do need the emerald." "Hear me out. The emerald only hid is trees; if the earth's core slows down the plants will die right after the people, the emerald will glow, grab them, get Sapphire, open the gate and then Eden's forest. Is there, we just got to be quick." "And where that leave us?" "We can't even leave Hell without the Lying Sin." 'We can't leave hell to earth idiot! We can just be in Eden's forest, only when someone is there, kind of like what happens to grandfather."

"Well, that does make sense." "Alright, attack the earth core it is."

"Wait, but what about the tree gate on earth, it'll die."

"Please, there are other gates on other planets, which have gates to the Eden forest, and it doesn't need life on earth; it depends on its own shit. Let's go."

"He makes a point, get the demons and attack earth's core," ordered Satan. On earth, Jesus warriors were walking through the park.

"Guys, you won't believe what happen."

"We know Abigail; we were there." "No, I'm talking about when I with the guardian of water. She was the guardian of water before I was, and she taught me all those things I can do with water now, and now I can control liquid too. Also, she said, Jesus is basically her creator." "And that means?"

"Who knows. We could be Jesus children, and get it we're Jesus warriors."

"That does make sense.... that could be true, we'll just ask Ida." Says Usher.

"Hey guys, look at the sheep. I wanna feed them. Give me a quarter." Says Sonny. Tristan gave him a quarter and he went to extend it for sheep food in the machine and started to feed the sheep. "Aww, so cute."

"You're in danger."

"What the-Uh Fairy of earth, please tell me that wasn't you."

"U know I can't be seen out in public, and no, that wasn't me."

"It was me. God of earth, the earth's core. I can sense it because I am an animal. The demons are attacking the earth's core."

"What...?" "You're the God of the earth; it will affect you too since you're not that strong enough to be immune to it."

"No way..." Then everything started to shake. "AHHH!" Sonny fainted. "Sonny? Sonny?!?" Yelled Roman. The earth's crust started to break, and the people were losing air. "It's the earth core." says the guardian of water. "Let's transform and save these people," says Roman. They transformed.

"Where is Sonny?" "Down there!" Pointed Sapphire. "Air!' The wind slowly picked up Sonny, and Allyson grabbed him.

"What's going on? It seems like the planet is getting destroyed," says Sashell.

"It's the core of the planet. The demons are attacking. "You guys go down there, we'll stay and keep the people alive," says E.J. They nodded.

"How are we going to go down to the earth's core?" "No need. VENUS, POWER!" A huge beam strikes down to the ground creating a huge whole. "This will lead to the earth's core, let's go," says Sashell. They went down there."

"Alright, Jesus warriors. Let's go," says Tristan. 'Air!' Shouted Usher.

A tornado has formed. "Water!" Shouted Abigail. A storm arrived wetting the floor. "ICE!" Shouted E.J. the ground was mobilized. "This will keep the planet on cracking, I hope the rest of them know what they're doing," says Gabriella. The rest of the group reached the earth's core, and what they saw was the demons attacking the core.

"What are they're doing?!"

"Don't they need something on this planet so their leader can come out, and the person who has the lying sin can't die," says Roderick.

"I don't know what's really going on, but we can't let them attack the core. Let's go," says Britannia. They flew in, stopping the demons.

"Guys...You have to let me go inside the core," says Sonny. "What? You won't survive." "Not in human.... form. Angel fairy!" "I'm on it." They transform, but he could barely fly. "Sonny...!" "No need. I just got to get to the core. I'll probably be like my older siblings." "And what if that Anti-Christ comes back?" Asked Allyson.

"Remember we got saved by someone and he never bothers following us. Let's go." The low key tried to sneak to the core. The warriors were attacking the demons. "You can't catch me, Zack."

"Oh, yes, I will." He attacks her, but she dodged. "Is that the best you can do?" Then Lucy spotted Allyson carrying a weak Sonny.

"Oh no, you don't!" She summoned a sphere and blasted it at them. Allyson noticed and used boom eggs to contour it. "No way you're carrying him into the core! HA!" She blasted another beam at them, but Allyson still used boom eggs to counter it.

"Guys, destroy the core, before the God of earth reached it!" Shouted Lucy. The demons stopped what they were doing and attacked the core. The God warriors used shield over their attacks.

"Hurry up and reached to the core before they destroy it." Says Meisha. "I'm surprised you can talk now Meisha, over 20 chapters." Says Sonny.

"Geez, fourth wall break?!" She shouted. "Of course!" says Allyson. She flew to the core, but Jade tries to stop them with another beam, and they got hit. Sonny was falling to the larva.

"SONNY!!" Yelled Junior!" He quickly pulled some rocks so that he won't fall to the larva.

"Ugh!" Max blasted dark spheres at him, but Sonny was rolling over to prevent getting hit. Sapphire flew up.

"Sun blast!" A huge yellow blast out of her, and it hit everyone.

"Sorry, guys." She used a yellow line and grabbed sonny. The demons started to attack, but the other warriors counter. Sapphire flew sonny into the core, and he was inside.

"NO!!" Yell all the demons. "Why didn't you do this before?" Asked Josh. "I have no idea. But he's in the core; I think the earth is not in his commands."

"Hell hand!" Yell one demon. A huge larva hand is coming straight towards Sapphire. She was about to dodge, but then it stopped like it was being controlled. "What the hell?" Says Glenn.

Then a huge shine approaches the sphere. "Earths and all the planets in the omniverse and behind it are in my Doman." He started to beat the demons up using earth's powers. The warriors quickly teleported out before they get hit.

"Seriously. What is up with us getting beaten?" Asked Winston. "Where's Sonny."

"He's basically everywhere. He's the earth," says Meisha.

"What?" Asked Abigail. "About time, you talked." Says Roman.

A huge dirt came out the dirt, and Tristan felt something. "Huh? The Larva is rising..."

"No, it's not..." "Huh? Who said that?" Asked Sashell. "It's me Sonny. I can connect to people's minds now since I am now the God of all earth, that's my new ability, and so are the Jesus warriors." He explained.

"Where are the demons?" Asked Shquana.

"They teleported. They're gone."

"Great they're gone, and we waste our day; it's close to sun set," says Gabriella.

"Quit your complaining." Says sonny as he controls the earth backward, and it's now in the afternoon. "What happens, it's-" "Yup. 4 o'clock."

Sonny was out of the core and appeared right in front of them. "Now even if the core got attack again, it won't really injure me. I can control it."

"Well, now that's out of the picture. Let's have some fun at the zoo." Says Abigail. They flew down and de-transform back.

Twenty-One

E.J. PART I

The Jesus warriors were ready to go to bed. "Wow, Sonny, can you really control all of the earths in existence." "Not really..." "What do you mean?" Asked Abigail.

"If I get to an omniverse level, I can even summon earth rocks from other verses, and I can even control gravity if I make it to another level."

"But that doesn't make any sense; we're in the omniverse; we should be omniverse level by now," says E.J.

"Not really, we're in still low come warriors; we're just becoming warriors now, we have only the gem Diamond. Who knows what other gems could be waiting out there?" says Gabriella.

"Wait, you can control Gravity? Who said?" "The woman back at the science fair, she says we have a second power match to our element power." "That is?" Asked Tristan.

"Tristan, you'll have light and Darkness, Roman will have Shadow, control people shadows, Usher will have Beast power, Abigail will have mind manipulation, I'll have Gravity, E.J. and Gabriella will have Beast power."

"Wait, why do Gabriella and I have the same power?" Asked E.J. "I think because Frost and Ice are almost as identical power and the fact that your full siblings due to the same mom and dad," says Usher.

"Wait, but that doesn't-wait the woman in my vision told me we're even half-siblings in our past lives, and she told me that Jesus is her creator. What if we're Jesus real children...?" Asked Abigail.

"You could be right... What is also the reason we're named after Jesus as his warriors, me, Roman, and Usher met the guy once, and I did see a man in some bright light over some blue fire kingdom," says Tristan.

"Could it really be true...are we really Jesus children." "We need answers; we're just assuming and making up theories." "Then why are we the only ones the Demons are mostly attacking and getting a great amount of power?" Asked Roman.

"Hey, Gabriella, and I didn't get power?" "That's true, who knows, you'll probably get it today and Gabriella tomorrow," says Sonny.

"Maybe we would be Jesus and the women in our visions...Could it be that those are our real mothers...?"

"Oh...Well..." "E.J. I got some great news," says their mother coming in. "What is it mom." "I got a letter, and you're going on a field trip to the ice ring."

ALL: "WHAT?!"

"Please tell me that the other grades are going with the 5th graders?" Asked Tristan.

"Do you really think high school students will go to a kid's field trip?" Asked Roman.

"Hey, I'm a good Ice skater," says Tristan. "Go to bed, you all got school in the morning," says Eric as he was walking by.

"Okay father, night you guys." They all went to bed, but before that, E.J. summoned his fairy angel.

"Hey, do you think I'm going to meet Jesus or the woman in my visions in my dreams?" "Who knows? Maybe it could be Jesus since it did happen with your older brothers."

"That could be true...I'm so excited that we're going to the ice ring too, but I'm not really a good ice skater, also did you heard about the new powers...I can't believe I'll get beast mode. I wonder what it'll be like."

"You did have it before." 'When?" "Back in the day before you were re-born along with the other warriors." "Was it badass, wait you were inside of me?"

"Of course, I was, I came out of you as soon as you were turned into a baby and your beats form is very fast and badass. It's

187

mixed with ice, and sometimes you fuse with your sister Gabriella to make a huge one."

"Now I really wanna see. I better get some sleep for the field trip tomorrow." He starts to get comfortable to get ready to sleep.

"Good night God of Ice." His fairy vanished. It was already daytime, and E.J. woke up. "Huh? What the-? I didn't meet Jesus or... The woman..."

"E.J. You up? Come on. It's time for breakfast, and you need to hurry up and get ready. The bus will be here." Says Abigail.

"Yeah. Okay." He got ready and started to eat his breakfast.

"Guys, we need to talk." "We'll talk when we're walking right now, just eat your breakfast..." Says Tristan. They were finished, and they head out. "So, what's up...?" Asked Roman.

"I didn't meet Jesus....Or the woman in my visions." "You're joking." "No, I'm not, maybe it's not my day..."

"You'll probably meet them while you're at the ice rink. Remember, you're being surrounded by ice, coincidence...?" Asked Tristan.

"That is true..." "And you'll probably meet them there like what happened to Abigail and me," says Sonny. "Yeah. Okay, you may be right." They were already at school. "Alright kids, we're going to the ice ring, did you bring the permission slips, and we're going with the 4th graders as well. 'Looks like Gabriella is going as well.' They reached to their book bags to give the permission slips, and then E.J. was in shocked, my permission slip...!"

"E.J.? Is there something wrong...?"

"Yes. It's just...I left my permission slip at home."

"Guess you won't go on the trip; you'll be with the high scholars."

"[GASPED]." In Hell, Satan was watching E.J. through his orb.

"Got a plan?" "Of course! It looks like his sister is going to the ice ring, let's slit this day up. Some demons attack the Ice ring and some attack the school. He's not surrounded by Ice; he'll get an achieve power like the others." "Great idea, but you do realize Gabriella will achieve one." 'It'll take time. Let's not forget we're just here for the lying sin or the capture of Sapphire. Sapphire will try to reach the ice ring to heal quickly. Capture her before she reaches the new form or prevents her from doing that." Demand Satan. "Of course, granddad. You all heard that?" Asked Lucifer Jr. The demons nodded in their lounge. On earth, E.J. was walking to the high school part. "At least I'm in Usher classroom. I'll try communicating with him. Usher? Usher?" He said in his mind calling his brother's name. 'E.J.? Aren't you supposed to be on the trip?' 'Yeah, but the thing is, I left my permission slip. There goes my chance on meeting the woman in my visions and Jesus, I'm going to be in your class.' 'You know you can just transform and fly to the ring and make sure you're not founded.' E.J. Stopped. 'Usher, you are a Genius! I love you so much!' He hummed in excitement. E.J. ran outside and towards a corner. "Angel. We still have time to go to the skating ring."

"But would you get caught?"

"Nope, not in human form. No one will bother a warrior of God.

Well, Jesus. Let's go." He transformed and followed the school bus to the ice rink.

"Man, so many children, now I'm kind of glad I'm not on the bus; the school bus to school and the home was enough." Then someone spotted him.

"Oh my God, a warrior!" He shouted. Then everyone spotted. E.J. waved. "Thank goodness they can only see a body of light, not my real identity." "E.J.? Whispered Gabriella.

'What was that, Gabriella?" Asked her friend.

"Oh, nothing." 'E.J. What the hell?" thought Gabriella connecting to him. 'Usher gave me a great idea, I'll just go to the Ice ring, and then there's my chance to-[GASPED]!' An attack was coming towards the bus, but E.J. created Ice to shield.

"Damn it." The demons with their clones were above. The bus drove super-fast. "Some of you followed the bus, it'll lead to Gabriella and attack when the target is alone, we'll deal with E.J. "Ugh! Damn you!" E.J. attack them with Ice shards, but they dodged. "Bad idea."

"Actually, that was a great idea," says Sapphire flying down with the rest of the warriors."

"Hmm, that's odd their only less of them," says Julmarie. They must be going after Gabriella! She's going to the Ice ring," says Usher.

"Us Marry warriors will go, you guys stay here, Sapphire come on." She nodded, and they flew, but the demons blasted at them.

"Hurry up guys and attack the target. The warriors know the plan. "Hmph fine." "AIR!" Shouted Usher as air blasted towards them. They used Fire's powers to prevent that. "Seriously?"

"Ugh!" They glowed yellow. "Looks like shits going down again." Says Zack. "ICE!" Shouted E.J. They got stabbed a bit.

"Damn it we let our guard down," says Glenn. Glenn came right after E.J. and blasted a dark blast very fast, but he dodged. Peter was behind him and kicked him down to the water. "AH DAMN IT!!" he shouted. Tristan used fire at both of them, and they got hit.

"Karma hit you both really good, don't mess with my brother!" E.J. was underwater. 'Damn it. If only I didn't-Wait.' He noticed he was in the water.

"I got it; maybe this is my chance to meet either of them." He froze all of the water, and it was turning into Ice. "Huh?" Asked Britannia in shocked.

"What's he doing?" Asked Meisha. "He's getting more power!" Yelled Peter clone.

The warriors stopped them from harming the ice. "Jesus...? Woman in my visions...? Any of you...?" "Turn around..." Says a voice.

Huh?" He turned around and spotted a woman covered in Ice. "[GASPED]." "Nice to see you again. E.J."

Twenty-Two

E.J. PART II

You did quite a nice job freezing the lake, what a smart move." "Actually I was originally supposed to meet you at the skating rink, but...[GASPED] My sister."

"No need, she'll be fine, but this time it's going to be different." "What do you mean? You'll see. She'll tell. But now you've got to learn how to really control your Ice powers." "Just one, actually two questions."

"That is?" "Why do my siblings and I need these powers to contain it. It's like it's more massive... It can like blew up a whole planet, even stop the Hell hand, and is Jesus really your creator?" "The first answer to your question is, you'll need it in the future, basically Season 3."

"Geez, fourth wall break?" "I'm sorry, I just like 4th wall breaks... [GIGGLES]. And the second to your answer is yes, Jesus is my creator."

"Then he must be your father, that must mean I'm the Messiah, right?" "Uh...We're wasting time. You need to control all the Ice."

"Yes, how do I do that...?" "It'll be easy. You did it in the past, so this won't be hard, and it wasn't hard for Abigail either." "What about my eldest three brothers?"

"They instantly learn it from Jesus because they used it more than you, Abigail, Sonny, and Gabriella, but it still won't be hard." "Okay, just tell me what to do," says E.J. Outside.

The demons try to escape to the ice ring, but the warriors prevented them. "Stay away from my sister, you freak!" says Britannia summoning an attack and blasting it at them. They dodged.

"You all don't know how to quit!" says Zack. "And so are you." Says Sashell above him, kicking him down, but he quickly vanished and was above her, but she vanished as well try to kick him, but he used force-field. She still kicked the force-field trying to break it. Then Junior arrived using laser eyes, then Roderick using White orbs, then Allyson with rainbow boom eggs, then lastly Shquana disappearing herself into petals raping around his force-field and explode while Sashell backed away, the force-field broke, and he got injured.

"Damn it! Ugh!" "Hmph." Then Jade came across using black orb towards them, but then Abigail used a water gun towards it, and it cost a huge explosion with steam. "Aww, man, I can't see anything...." Says Shquana.

Then Zack came towards them, blasting a huge beam at them, but then Roderick used a shield. Then all of a sudden it started to snow. "Snow? Why is it snowing?"

"Could this be E.J.?" Asked Meisha. "That's impossible; he can only control Ice. Snow is not Ice, that means it could be-" says Tristan.

Under the frozen Ice river, E.J. felt something really freezing. "This feeling, what is this?" "Snow...?" "In summer?" "No, not any snow...It's Gabriella; this is your chance to speed things up." says the Ice woman.

"Okay." Outside. Zack tries to destroy the storm, but the warriors prevent them from doing that as well. "Which one warrior? The sky? Or the lake?!" Yelled Zack's twin! "I'm your opponent, you little shit!" says Sashell as she flies kicked him away.

"Ugh, Damn you." Aleg attack the river, but Tristan quickly fly to the Ice, skate across to the attack, and used fire shield so it won't touch the Ice. "Come on E.J. we can't keep this up. They can duplicate themselves, and we'll totally be outmatched. Come on!"

"Right here, Tristan." said a voice. "Huh?" The Ice started to shake.

"What the-Oh Crap!" He quickly flew up with the rest of the warriors and used a shield with them; then in an instant, all the planet was covered in Ice. The warriors couldn't believe their eyes on what they have seen. "What the... What's going on? Is this whole place a giant Ice kingdom?" Asked Meisha.
"Yes, but the whole planet is." Says E.J. Flying up in his power form like his siblings had. "E.J.? Oh, my God. This is wow..." says

Roman. "But I had a little help." He turned around, seeing Gabriella flying towards them.

"Gabriella...Wait, where's the Marry warriors with Sapphire." "On the moon." "Wait...What? How? Actually...what?" Asked Rihanna.

"Yeah, When I achieve this form, I made it snow, even without meeting the woman in my dreams, or Jesus. My power just shines, and I made it snow, and with the power of E.J. ice, the whole planet just turned into an Ice kingdom."

"The people." Says Sashell. "Eh, we'll just revive them," says E.J.

"Guys! OMG guys, you wouldn't believe it. We were in space, and it's so beautiful, and the planet looks like two circles in one."

"Of course, we're in the multiverse, and I can tell even space is green, yellow, and black?" Asked Gabriella.

"Yeah, how did you." "I saw a picture of the multiverse while my powers were rising. Now lets' turn this puppy back to normal." "But first, we're the demons."

"They must've escaped; we'll deal with them later." 'Aww great and just to think I wanted to beat up Lucy more for what she did to me at the ring and to my friend, she nearly died, if Sapphire hasn't healed quickly."

"Well, at least she's alive, come on." Says E.J., they vanished the Ice and it was back to normal."

"Revival." Says all the other remaining Jesus warriors. Everyone was living again. "Erased." says the God Warriors.

Everything was like it never happened. "Let's get home," says Sapphire.

Twenty-Three

GABRIELLA POWER
OF SNOW

During the fight with the demons, the school bus was being driven quickly because of the incident. "Oh my God, I thought we were goners." says a boy.

"So, this is how the people felt back in the centuries? Damn," says Gabriella's friend named Rachel. Gabriella was staring at the window wondering about her brother. "Hey, Gabriella, is everything alright?" asked Rachel.

"Oh yeah. I'm just a little shocked that we nearly got killed." The school bus finally arrived at the rink.

"Okay Kids, straight line and we got to go to the ring," says their teacher. They were in a straight line and they walk inside. 'Come

197

on. Come on. I need to go and help the warriors,' says Gabriella in her thoughts. They walked inside and Gabriella tries to sneak out. "Gabriella, where are you going?" 'Oh...Uh. I need to go use the bathroom."

"We say do anyone has to go used the bathroom before we left, we got a message saying the bathroom won't be fixed until noon." "Noon?"

"You have to hold it until it's done. Sorry about that." "It's okay. I'll hold." They started to put on their shoes.

'I got to figure out a way. The warriors need me, Damn. I should've stayed with E.J." Whispered Gabriella. 'What was that, Gabriella?" Asked Rachel.

"Oh, it's nothing." She got up. Rachel nearly slipped because of the skating shoes, but Gabriella captures her.

"How do you walk in these shoes? I really wish we went to the roller rink." "Still the same thing." She replied with a smile.

"Can you skate with me?" 'Uh...Well." She was thinking about the warriors. "[SIGH]. Yeah. Sure." They walked to the skating rink, and they begin to skate."

"How are you so good at skating at a young age?' "Well, I'm only 10, and I just know how to skate, probably cause of my mother." "Oh..."

"Hey, Rachel, you need to help me get to the bathroom." "Why? Do you really need to go that badly?" "Well. I just need to do something?"

"What a number 2...?"
"Uh..." She started to sweat and blush. "OMG, what did you ate girl?"

"[CHUCKLED NERVESOULY]" "Come on..." They skate towards the out of the ring.

"Where do you think you're going?" asked a teacher standing at the edge of the ring, putting his hand out to stop the girls.

"Well, you see Mr. Odin. We just want to change our skates." "The skates seem fine to me."

"I just need to read my lucky book." "And this book, you should've read it during the bus."

"If I did, then everyone will laugh at me." "And what's this book name?" "It's special." "I don't believe you; you're lying." Then an attack came, and it hit Rachel right in front of Gabriella, which lead her in huge shocked on what's happening to her friend.

"[GASPED]." Her heart came out, and it showed no dark special sin. "Oh pity, no lying sin. Hmm?" says Lucy flying down.

"Oh, look it's Gabriella. Transform your son of a bitch, and let's fight!" She demanded. Everyone was shocked and looking at Gabriella in confused. "What she's a warrior?" asked a boy.

"The demon is talking to her saying to fight her, so she maybe is a demon."

"Oh, Damn. Guys! Get out of here! I'll just make the God warriors erased their memories. Angel fairy, let's transform." She transformed and flew up, and everyone was in shock.

"You heard the girl, let's leave!" Yelled a teacher. They ran. Lucy summoned a string tied around Gabriella's leg and dash her around the stadium seats like a rag doll. "AH!!!" She yelled in pain as she crashed. "This string... Then the Marry Warriors arrived with Sapphire.

"Lucy!" Yelled Winston coming straight at her, but then Lois came and kicked him down. She and the other demons except Lucy duplicated themselves due to Fire's red aura power.

"So that's how you guys wanna play? Boost!" says Sapphire.

The Warriors were glowing yellow even more. "You bitch! You're going to pay for that," says Winston as he grabbed her leg and swung her hard up. All the Marry warriors started to fight the demons and their clones. Sapphire flew down with Julmarie, but then an attack came, but Julmarie used a shield.

"Leave the victim and give Sapphire to me." Demanded Glenn clone!

"Like that's ever going to happen. Sapphire, go down."

"Nope! HELL HAND!" Yelled Peter clone. The hell hand came up trying to grab Sapphire, but then, Sheldon used an attack, and then Serena and Selena used a full attack power, and it got destroyed.

"No! UGH!" Yelled Peter clones as he went after them. "Julmarie, the victim."

"Damn it; this is going to be hard. I can't leave you alone."

"Wait, you can. The Hell hand only comes out once. It won't come out again."

"No. Just stay with me. Just a little longer." Lucy then pulls the string towards her as Gabriella came straight towards her, and then Lucy kneed her in her stomach, but then Gabriella quickly grabbed her leg and flipped her body up and kicked her in the face.

"You Bitch!" She then swings her down to the ice rink. "You moron!" Yelled Glenn. A huge Ice started to freeze the String, but Lucy quickly snapped it out, but then Re-Re appeared behind her and kicked her to the ring. Gabriella flew up quickly and punched her in the face. Then she hit her with a frost attack and Lucy fell down. Then Lucy clone appeared behind Gabriella, but Gabriella quickly used a shield, but then Peter clone appeared and punched her to the stadium chairs, but she quickly landed but was a little injured.

"Damn..." "Gabriella..." Says Sapphire flying to her. "Sapphire...You need to stay with Julmarie.

"Not while you're injured. Let me heal you." "My friend. I'll be fine, go and heal my friend, since your escape from Julmarie. I'll be fine." As she said, grabbing her arm. Then Gabriella had a strange feeling.

"What the-" It showed a woman in a frost kingdom with Jesus as they turned around looking at Gabriella.

"Who are they...?" She then was in shocked and quickly flew to the Ice ring. 'What the-Gabriella!" Shouted Sapphire. 'She went there so instantly."

"You're all alone Sapphire, you're mine!" says Glenn clone. Sapphire flew up and began to fly away. "LEAVE ME ALONE!!!" She summoned her sun rod and threw it at him. Gabriella begin to fuse with the Ice, and it turned into snow.

"You're dead, Gabriella!" Yelled Lucy. "Never underestimate a Jesus warrior!" She shouted. Lucy begins to have a flashback at the same time she faced Gabriella when she first achieves this form way back then.

"N-No...." says Lucy in shocked. Gabriella begins to glow, and the Ice ring began to swarm her up. It shoots to the sky, and then a huge storm appeared. It was snow.

"Huh? Snow!!" Then a huge wind blasted the Marry warriors with Sapphire as soon as she was done healing Rachel. They were all the way at the moon. 'W-What the-Where are...we...?" Asked Cory. "We're at the moon," says His older sister Selena.

"Oh my God, this is so beautiful... look at space. It's like moonlights never ends...." says Sheldon. "And why is the earth so huge from the moon, and there are two circles closed together."

"Duh, we're not in a universe or any multiverse. We're in the omniverse, the verse of all creation," says Julmarie. "Uh, guys... Why the hell is the sky turning gray, like all over?" Asked Xavier.

"I think this is what Gabriella is doing, all because of me." "Huh? What do you mean? Why says that?" Asked Ally. "Because when she touched me, she had the same facial expression as when Tristan touched me back at his school, and she instantly flew to the Ice ring...I think she contains a new power. The form like Tristan and the others had." says Sapphire.

"I can't wait to hear her story," says Winston. They flew to earth. Gabriella was in her form, and the demons were in shocked.

"Crap! Aww man!" Says Lucy's twin. "Pay back, you little shit!" She shouted at Lucy. Lucy was completely paralyzed.

"What the hell? I can't move." "Frostbite. I injected it in you the moment Re-Re kicked you towards me. Now!' She attacked all of them with her snow attack and it blasted them off, she stepped outside and noticed the whole planet was covered in snow and Ice.

"Wow. An Ice kingdom. And I can feel it all over the planet, and I didn't do it alone. E.J. Thanks for your help. Sadly, I didn't really meet the woman in my visions or Jesus, but at least I saw them...Abigail's theory could be right."

She flew to where the warriors are at the Connecticut River. "Also, thank you Sapphire. I have been pulled into the Ice by someone, maybe by the woman or Jesus. I'll get my answer."

Twenty-Four

RAGE

The warriors arrived home, and it was already 3 p.m. At the Jesus warriors' house, they were in Gabriella's room.

"Well, at least school is over, and we all have that form! Too bad we won't get it again."

"We may will. The woman in my vision says so, and also...Abigail, I think your theory is right. I think we are Jesus children.

"What makes you think that?"

"The woman did say Jesus created her, and we could be his children." 'That does make sense, but guys, we got to focus on the biggest picture. It's almost the end of this season and the lying sin could be close, and we all have that form, the battle could be tuff." Says Roman. "Ugh, I hate fourth wall breaks, and true, we all have that form, and it's gone," says Usher.

"Look at the bright side, at least we're getting it back, and have Sapphire's sun boost in case they'll use Fire's attack, now I wonder who they'll attack next," says Sonny. In Hell, Satan was really pissed.

"Damn, two episodes at the same time where my demons get beaten, and now the last two had that fucking form!"

"Now, the battle will get good since they won't use that form again for a long time."

"I have an idea," says Firia coming up. "Oh hello, messiah," says Lucifer Jr. arriving with his twin brother Satan Jr.

"You fools are forgetting the lying sin could shine with the sun's power. If Sapphire were in a rage, the sun would double its light, kind of turning it into a red sun, the lying sin will have a huge shine, and there's your target, but you have to do it tomorrow." "What, why?"

"Because the demons will be badly injured from Sapphire's rage, she'll also use the trinity that's inside of her. The Father."

"Pff, that will be hard, how the hell are we going to get Sapphire in rage, and you can use Reality bending why can't you just summoned her here."

"Then there won't be more seasons and episodes if Sapphire was already here, and you guys act like you're not going to get her in Season 4." 'Alright enough with the 4th wall breaks!" Shouted E.J. outline.

"Piss off!" Yell Firia. "AH!" He fell down.

"Now, it was back to normal.

"Are we done? Can we continue this chapter? Okay. Fine, what's your plan?" Asked Satan. She smirked. On earth, the warriors were running to the school.

"How could we forget about our school bags?" Asked Abigail. "Hello? We were fighting demons," says E.J. "Guys, I think we should just wait until Tomorrow. It's Monday, and we don't have any valuable things in there."

"Well, you're probably right and they are in our lockers." Says Roman. "The teachers will be worried about us," says Roman. "The God Warriors erased their memories," says E.J.

"Oh yeah, that's right." Then a huge explosion accrued. "Oh, come on! Another one?" The Jesus warrior flew towards the destination and met up with the rest of the warriors flying.

"Now, who are they attacking." They arrived at the park. "The demons...! Alright, you guys already know the answer, you're not getting Sapphire and the fight will end up with us beating you, and we can tell you fail on capturing the person who had the lying sin," says Sashell.

"Oh please, we're not going to attack, we're just here to lure you in on something to see someone dearly we don't need anymore, Sapphire should take her place," explained Glenn. "Huh? What do you mean?" Asked Sapphire in shocked. "A little message from Fire," says Lucy. They glowed red and it showed a glowing screen. "Huh?" They all said. It showed a ceremony. Then it showed Firewalking in injured bruises.

'What the hell? No, this can't be..." says Roderick.

"Any last words weakling, Sapphire will be great down here since she possessed more powerful power than you for Satan's plan," says Satan Jr. "Who is that...?" Asked Britannia.

"Sapphire...Take care, and please don't get captured. I love you..." says Fire crying with a smile looking at the screen. "No... No...." The demons kicked Fire down the larva, and she been killed. Everyone was in shocked.

"Now then, give us Sapphire, or we'll be nice to retrieve her back," says Glenn. "You Bastard! How can you do something like that?!" Yelled Sheldon. "And you really think we'll give you Sapphire after what you did to her sister?!" Asked Re-re in raged.

"Fire...Come on...I need to contact you... If you don't tell me what Satan's is up too, then we'll never defeat him. The Jesus Warriors don't have their form anymore, and it'll be tuff. I need you...." says Sapphire walking slow and talking psychopathically.

"Oh, Sapphire..." Whispered Sashell as she was in shock. "Fire...please. This is a joke right...?" She started to tear up and burst out crying calling her name. "FIRE!!!!!!" Then she started to glow brightly; a symbol arrived on her head which was The Father power. "What is that symbol?" Asked Rihanna. "This power... It's intense!!!" Yelled Serena.

"You guys.... made one...huge...MISTAKE!!!" Yelled Sapphire as she lifts up her head in rage towards the demons. Her eyes were glowing red with tears, and a huge amount of aura blasted out of her. Everyone has been swept away.

"Guys, Fire aura!" says Lucy. They glowed red.

"Guys, Yellow aura," says Josh. They both glowed, but Sapphire's aura was so strong it vanished the aura right out of them and each of the group crashed. Sapphire aura begins to rap her, and it expands. "No, this is going to be like last time in episode 4 and 5," says E.J. The group was in shocked on what they're seeing coming out of Sapphire.

"Sapphire...." says Britannia, all worried. Sapphire looks directly at the demons and they're stomach been cut off. "Damn it!" Shouted the demons. "Holy shit! And it took just one look?!" asked Josh. "AAAAAHHHHH!!!!" Yelled Sapphire in rage, the sky started to turn darker, and the sun started to turn redder.

"The Sun! It's getting redder! And bigger!" Pointed Brandon. "No! It's coming closer!" says Rihanna.

"Oh my God, the sun is going to gulp the planet." Says Roderick.

"Earth!" Shouted Sonny. He tried to move the earth away from the sun, but it didn't work. "What's going on? Damn it; it's the gravity of The Sun," explain Sonny.

"No need! Air!" Shouted Usher as he controlled it to push the planet away from The Sun, but it was still no use. "It's Sapphire. Her gravity pull is too strong for us." Says Usher.

"We need to go. If we stay..." says Shquana.

"Guys, we need to exit the planet," says Roderick. 'No...I won't." says Britannia. "Britannia!" shouted Abigail.

"Britannia, I'm sorry," says Sashell grabbing her sisters in tears as they were flying away. They looked up and the sun was about to burn away the planet. "Damn it!" Shouted Tristan.

"Tristan, use your Firepower!" Shouted Trishawna.

"I can't! I tried, but it doesn't seem to work. Sapphire's power is too strong for me to maintain that firepower, and remember we're reborn, if I were me back then, I'd probably be able to handle it... I think." He explains. Sapphire ran towards the demons, but they quickly vanished. The sun crashed into the planet, but in an instant, the sun was away from the earth, but the temperature dropped, Sapphire was still in a rage after seeing her sister killed. Everyone was on the clouds, but they can still see Sapphire's huge amount of yellow aura.

"What's going on? I thought we were goners." Says Monica. "Nope, you been saved by us," says Ida appearing with the other supreme angels like her and the most famous idol Michael Danderson. "Ida! Wait, is that Michael Danderson? OMG!" Says Serena.

"Wait, he's concentrating," says Ida. "There's no time to go gaga over the Idol, both Sapphire and the sun are in danger, plus the planet, it's away from The Sun, close enough towards Saturn." says a Supreme angel.

"Wait. What? You know how cold that is? The people will die!" says Sheldon. "We know, but we'll revive whoever gets killed,

Also, it's thanks to Sapphire's aura that's keeping the earth nice and warm. Remember, she is the guardian of The Sun.

"Guys, this is my triplet sister Narada."

"Hello?" She responded. "Hello." They respond back. "I stopped the sun crashing to the planet; I used my Father power."

"Father power? Wait, the trinity power? One of them?"

"Yes. This is Serita the oldest Triplet." "Hello. My sister and I also possessed the Trinity power. I used my father's power to stop the sun colliding with the earth, but we are far away. And to be honest, Fire's not dead."

"She's not?!" They all said in shock. "No, that was an illusion created by Firia."

"Firia? That wicked son of a- [SIGH] never-mind. How are we going to stop Sapphire?" Ask Abigail. "No need. Fire is going to contact us now," says Starfiria summoning an orb as Fire was there.

"Fire." Says all the warriors. "Hey, guys. [GASPED]" She gasped as she sees her sister in a rage with huge amount of yellow aura.

"Sapphire, to think she became in a rage because of me...."

"Wait, you seem you're not in your cage," says Junior.

"That's because Starfiria, disguised as Firia, led me out and I escape." It showed a flashback. Fire was under the control of her aunt's aura and she couldn't really move. She couldn't even contact Sapphire. She heard footsteps coming her way and it was her aunt, but the aura was different. "Huh?" The door was open as she walked past it and vanished. 'This aura...' Then the red aura vanished. "The red aura from Fire vanished.

"Starfiria...Thank you." She escaped her cell. A few minutes after Satan, Jr. walked to her cell and noticed she was gone. 'What the hell? That bitch escaped!' The alarm went off.

"Oh, no." Whispered Fire. "ALERT! FIRE HAS ESCAPED HER CAGE! FIND HER!!!" Demand Satan. The demons went on out on finding her. Fire hid and contacted the warriors and angels. That was the end of the flashback. "I have to keep my lower power down so that they won't track me, and you have to save my sister."

"Remember Sapphire is a newcomer warrior like you all if she has never been reborn, it won't injure her badly. If Sapphire can't calm down, the whole earth and sun will be exploded as long with the solar system." Explain Starfiria.

"Will we die?"

"No." Replied Serita. "Oh, thank God."

"But you'll wonder around space for a long time and you won't know what's going to happen in the future, but there are the Jesus warriors, they can rebuild the earth back to the way it was." Says Ida. They smiled.

"I have an idea. We lost our perfect form for us Jesus warriors, but you possessed the Trinity power. You can fight with Sapphire one on one," says Tristan. "That is true, but she also has the Holy Spirit inside of her, well something in her possessed that power."

"Wait, you mean somebody is in Sapphire?" Asked Rihanna. She nodded. "Sealed up in her, but you'll meet her one day. Alright, I'll take her on." Serita dashed in."

Sapphire noticed her, and she jetted towards her. They collided their arms very badly, causing a huge sound wave.

"Sapphire...Calm down..." days Serita. Sapphire put more pressure onto herself causing Serita to crash down, but she landed and it a quick second she appeared behind Sapphire, trying to kick her down, but her kick went right through her. Serita backed up, but then Sapphire used the sun's power to sneak her from behind, and she got injured badly.

"Ugh!" "Serita!!" Shouted her sisters. Sapphire floated down and grabbed her head and begin to cry; then, her aura color changed to blue.

"Tristan then begins to become paralyzed. "Tristan?" Asked Roman and Shquana in shocked. "Sapphire started to see flashbacks. She sees Fire and another girl who looks exactly like her. They were on a red planet, then a royal ball on a gas giant.

She sees Firia in her Son power against a powerful opponent at the royal ball. Then she sees herself in bed with both of them holding her hand. She then sees Firia being taken away by the dark. "You're next, Sapphire," said a voice behind her. She turned around and it was Lucifer Jr. grabbing her.

"[SCREAMS]!!" Serita backed up. More energy was coming. "What are we supposed to do? Stand here and do nothing?"

"Not exactly." "What do you mean?" "It'll take about 7 hours until Sapphire blew up the planet due to the state she's in, but if she were the warrior she was before she was reborn, she'd destroy even the whole omniverse faster than a blink of an eye."

"No way." They all said. "It is true."

"Guys, you must know, Satan can't kill me because he needs me for his plan. He needs both Sapphire and me. You got to tell Sapphire I'm alright."

"Fire behind you! Satan, Jr." Says Cory.

"[GASPED]!" The glowing screen vanished. "Oh, no!" Yelled Roderick. "Relax. Remember they can't kill her, and Satan Jr. will do something really amazing," says Starfiria.

In Hell, Fire was backing up. "Stay away from me. What you're doing to my sister was really out of your head and nothing but an illusion created by my aunt."

"Just shut the hell up, I can't believe I'm doing this, but I'm gonna help you reached to your cage safely."

"I don't believe you..." "I can't watch you get punished by my grandfather or my father or uncles. Let's go."

He grabbed her and ran, but then he hid back once the guards were running across.

"You just had to run away out your cage, why the hell didn't you contact them through cage?"

"Because...I never really see most of hell. I have been in that cage for 800 years." "Oh, you stupid Fuck." He sees the coast is clear and ran towards the cell. 'I can't believe it...Maybe deep in his hard, he is a nice person due to his mom...' On earth, Julmarie looked at everyone as they were worried about their friend/ Family member. He walked towards, and Starfiria smiled. He dashed down. "Julmarie!" Yelled all the Marry warriors. "Sapphire, I'm coming to save you."

He flies past Serita and she was a little shocked. Sapphire spotted Julmarie and attack him. He dodged and flew down.

"Sapphire, you got to-AH!" She hit him with a sunbeam.

"Damn...Sapphire!!!" He shouted. "FIRE!!!" She shouted in tears. Tristan was still paralyzed.

"Starfiria...Please...Help him," says Sonny. She nodded her head, and Tristan was un-paralyzed.

"Whoa, that was fast...How did she..." "There's something off about her...Her power...is... Godlike..." says Tristan. Britannia was staring at Michael as he was closing his eyes. 'I wonder what's he's concentrating, well I shouldn't be distracted — my sisters in trouble. Then a light appeared above them and it was a sword. "What the-What did he just drove...?" Asked Josh. "A Holy sword. he is now capable of summoning and using Holy Swords," says Ida. "Holy Swords? I heard of them, but I thought those were myths," says Selena.

"Nope, they're real." He vanished. "Aww, he went away."

"No, he been summoned back by Jesus himself; he was here because Jesus knows he'll summon the sword thanks to Sapphire's light." Explain Ida. Down on the ground, Julmarie was pushing his way in through Sapphire's huge amount of aura.

"Sapphire...Listen to me!! Fire is not dead!" He shouted. Sapphire was still crying. "It was just an illusion. Satan will not kill her; he needs her for his plan. So, calm down, Sapphire...SHE'S ALIVE!!! PLEASE COME BACK!!!" He shouted. Sapphire looked at him and her aura power broke. She fainted, but he caught her.

"J-Julmarie...?" "You're back...Sapphire...Don't scare me like that ever again..." "W-What happened...? [GASPED], w-what happened. Did I really do all of this?" "Yeah, those demons tricked you and got into you, thinking they kill Fire, but she's not dead."

"Well, at least I hope so. I really hope Satan Jr. didn't do anything to her.' He thought. "I just read your mind." "What now?" "Relax Sapphire," says Starfiria walking to her.

"Who-[GASPED]. This energy. Its God likes." "I am Starfiria. Jesus' sister." They both were in shock. "WHAT?!"

"You need to tell me you're the messiah?" 'Of course. Fire is safe. I can see she's safe in her cell; Satan Jr. didn't do anything to her." In Hell, Satan Jr. quickly returned her back to her Cell.

"You know I can tell you had teleportation; you could've wished your ass back without going through that stupid drama.

"Yeah, but...it was nice of you doing something really nice." "I'm not nice. I just enjoy torturing you, and no one else. Just me." He locked the cage and vanished.

"[CHUCKLED]." She chuckled, blushing a bit. On earth, Sapphire got up.

"Thank you for doing that for my sister." She nodded.

"Well, angels, we need to go to heaven, and as for this." It was quickly fixed up and the sun was back to normal.

"Whoa, so Godly fast." Says Sapphire. "Good-bye." She bowed down as she and the angels disappeared.

"Oh, my God. I'm so sorry you guys." "Hey, it's okay, normally sisters will go crazy if they're sisters are killed right in front of them, actually any family members."

"[CHUCKLED." Yeah, let's get back home. My mom's cooking spaghetti." Says Sapphire.

ALL: "Yeah." and they cheered and flew off.

In Hell Satan finally found the woman. It's here...Finally, it's here the sin is glowing thanks to the red sun, it'll shine forever, tomorrow morning makes the demons attack her real quick so that the warriors won't intervene." Commanded Satan!

"Yes, Father. Demons! Since the other demons are badly injured, you guys will be the one to get the lying sin." It showed 14 nameless demons who were buff. "Shits really going to get real."

Twenty-Five

THE SIN IS FOUND!
BATTLE ON PART I

The Jesus warriors were ready to go to bed. "Man, that meatball and Spaghetti was absolutely delicious from Aunty Yanique," says Roman.

"I can't believe I waste my school trip, talk about annoying Satan is coming after the person who has the lying sin," says Gabriella.

"I always wonder, are we really going to be doing this for the rest of our lives? No matter who Satan attacks we'll always be there to stop him, it's getting annoying and we're on chapter 24/episode 24," says E.J.

"You're such a hypocrite. You're saying it's not okay for 4th wall breaks but, here you're doing a 4th wall break," says Usher.

"Maybe because you guys keep doing, I'm doing it so this episode can go faster." He replied, laying down. "I always wonder...Who has the lying sin?" Asked Abigail.

"Not even us know, and I doubt our angel fairies will tell us." Says Tristan. "I doubt they even know." Says Sonny. "We're so going to beside characters once it reaches to season 2, 4, 5, 6, 7."

"What the hell, you know what. Who cares about these 4th wall breaks? Christian siblings have so many 4th wall breaks." "Of course, they're messiah's, Gods," says Roman.

"Wait, I have a theory," says Tristan. "What could that be?" Asked Usher. On Earth, the nameless buff demons were at their target. "So, this is the target...?" says one.

"Yes..." During the Jesus warriors' time, "I think, the lying sins comes from a person who a Satanist...?"

"You could be right, they could say Satan sin me," says Abigail. "No way, he's their God, there's no way he's going to give his worshippers what they want."

"Wait, how come in this season it's mainly about us, but as E.J. quote, we're going to beside characters...?" Asked Usher.

"That is true, and they are lying sin has to be bigger, I saw every time Sapphire heal the victims. When I see their heart, it's tiny spots..." "And Satanist people don't show themselves during daylight, and they mostly dress black or Goth."

"That's a lie; they're some Christians who dress as Goth."

"Wait, since this season focuses on us, and those women in our dreams and visions, those could be our mothers," says Sonny.

"I just remembered, didn't mom dress as Goth one day and she's a pure Christian, and she says, 'I don't care let them sin me' before when we were younger when she was drinking Achole and we beg her to stop and take off those Goth clothing?"

"Holy crap, I never thought of that; we were young," says Gabriella. Then there was a knock on the door.

"Guys, you got dirty clothes," says their mother. Then Usher senses something in the air.

"They're HERE!" He shouted. Then a demon blasted in and attacked the warriors, Sonny used the ground as a shield, but they broke it, but they quickly got out.

"Mom!" Yelled Gabriella. "What the hell is that?" Asked Their mother. "There's the target!" shouted one. The Jesus warriors carried their mom into the bathroom.

"Mom, promise you won't tell anyone about this or get shocked." "What do you mean? What's going on?" Then the demon opened the door. Sonny broke the wall and created steps out of trees. Abigail summoned water out of their pipes and blasted towards them.

"These demons, they look different," says Abigail. "They're probably new ones. Let's go," says Sonny.

They ran down the steps. The demons rushed through the water. "So, I see, they can use their powers without transforming," says One demon. "It's because they're protecting their 'Mother.""

"The demons walked down the steps, but sonny. Dissolved them! "You're so forgetting we can fly." Says One demon. "AIR!!" Yelled Usher. A huge tornado gulps them up.

"Go on! Transform!" "I don't think we need to transform. We're using our powers without transforming, how come?" Asked Tristan.

"That's because you guys learn how to use your powers without transforming, even without us," says Angel fairy of Fire. "How is that possible...?" Asked Gabriella.

"Remember the woman in your visions, to be honest. Those are your mothers, and that ability you guys learn when you had your own episode, it all transfer to your human form, and you can now use your power without transforming." Explain Angel of air.

"You know what? Let's keep this a secret among the other warriors, and they want in, also we're going to be pretty good sacrifices in season 3, and we want to be fair with the warriors." Says Roman.

"Also, in Christian Showdown Season 3, we'll use our powers without transforming there," says Usher. 'Geez, so much 4th wall breaks." says Angel of Earth.

"We're going to get used to it, besides there's no 4th wall breaks during the future seasons, not even once."

"Oh. Okay." "Guys, don't tell me..."

"Yes, mom. We're the Jesus warriors."

"I've always known. I've seen seven infant babies at my door, and I took care of them; each started to grow, but not at the same time. You guys now often go in your room whispering and stuff...You guys were different...Even if you guys are the warriors, I'll still-" "Mom, look out!" Yelled Abigail. A demon smashes his hand through Neata's back to her heart. "BASTARD!!!" Yelled E.J.

"Snowstorm!!!" Yelled Gabriella, and it started to snow hard. The demons tried to see but couldn't."

"Finally, the Lying sin is ours-! AAHH!" Yelled the demon as he was getting kicked by Roman.

The sin was falling, and the demons plus the warriors were getting it.

"AIR!" Called out Usher as air controlled the sin coming towards him. A demon attacked usher, and he lost control of his air powers. "Damn it!" The sin begins to fall.

"SNOW!" Yelled Gabriella as the snow hits everyone.

"Lightning!" Shouted Roman as he controls lighting hitting the demons, but they quickly healed. "What kind of demons are they?" Asked Gabriella.

"I don't know, but they're tuff. WATER!" Abigail blasted water towards them to keep them away from the sin. "I got it!" Yelled Tristan.

"No, you don't." shouted another.

"EARTH!" Shouted Sonny as he put his other hand out as he was holding his mother along with E.J. A huge stone came up holding the sin and it was coming straight towards Tristan. The demons blasted at E.J. and Sonny. "Lightning!" says Roman as Lightening came out of his hands." It hit the blast. "Tristan grabs it," says E.J. Tristan was about to grab it, but then he was pushed

221

back instantly to the ground. "What the hell was that?" He looked up and was in huge shocked that it was the Anti-Christ."

"No, not you again," says Tristan. "It is, and I believe that lying sin is mine."

He started to control earth, and Sonny was parlayed. "Sonny?

"What's going on? How is he controlling Earth, while Sonny is the God of earth," says Abigail? "Ice!" Yelled E.J.

"That won't work against me E.J." He started to control Ice, and E.J. was paralyzed.

"I see, he's stronger than us, that's why. He carries Satan's blood in him. Guys don't attack him, or he'll possess you." says Roman dashing around. "Hmm, it looks like you have no choice but to stay there while I get the lying sin." 'Ugh...' says all the Jesus warriors. Then an attack came. It went right through the Anti-Christ. It hit the Sin, and it landed a few meters away from Tristan.

"[GASPED]. "Gasped Tristan. The Anti-Christ looked up and the rest of the warriors was coming in. "Sashell...Hm? Where the hell is Sapphire?"

"None of your business." The Anti-Christ appeared right in front of her face and slammed her to the ground. "Sashell!"

They all yelled. "You guys join her." He demanded, and they all gone crashed down, but Sonny used earth and made it soft to cushion their fall, including Sashell's.

"You guys, okay?" Asked Roman flying down.

"What it looks like? Thanks to your brother." Says Winston sarcastic. "Seriously, where is Sapphire?" Asked Roman.

"She's at the house in a deep slumber, I tried to wake her up, but she wouldn't wake up, the demons are still after her, so we left her there with Roderick." Explain Britannia.

"I heard that. HA!" Yelled the Anti-Christ. He dashed to Sapphire's house.

"No!" They all yelled. Then the Marry warriors have been summoned. "Huh? Where did they go?!" Asked Junior.

"Where did Sashell go?" Asked Britannia. Then Sashell grabbed the sin as everyone was distracted and battling the Jesus warrior from above. It was glowing like crazy.

"No!" Yell the Anti-Christ. He dashed towards her instantly, but then Tristan used fire shield, and she quickly flew away, but the Anti-Christ broke his shield and injured him badly, he was coming straight towards her, but then, he had a huge feeling and he acted up and fell down hard.

"What the-" Says Sashell. "Give us the lying sin!" Yelled the demons coming after her. The God warriors attack them, but they dodged still going after her. Britannia appeared right before Sashell and used canon rocks at them, and they got hit.

"AIR!" Shouted Usher. A huge tornado approaches them and gulps them up.

"Ice!" Shouted E.J. as he froze the tornado with the demons inside, but it begins to crack.

"Damn it. These demons are Tougher than the ones we fought. I'll keep using Ice, Usher what are those other powers we have." "I forgot, but even if I knew, we wouldn't be using them until we're on the next level."

"Oh, we're on the next level, alright." The Anti-Christ was struggling to get up. "What's up with him?" Asked Rihanna flying with Allyson.

"Don't know. Dusk this bitch!" Says Junior.

"Dave...Zeus...What are you doing here...?" He whispered. Usher turned around as he heard the Anti-Christ whispered.

"Dave...Zeus? Who's that? Wait...Jesus Brother...?" Asked Usher in shocked.

"What? Jesus' brother is here?" In hell, Satan was watching through his orb.

"Damn it! That son of a bitch Zeus is o the omniverse earth. Now the Anti-Christ 1 is weakened by his sent alone! DAMN IT! DAMN IT! DAMN IT!!! Ugh!!! Maybe I should send my omniverse Gods, and oh wait, they're still weaker against Zeus. Ugh! Someone just get the Lying Sin before it's too late!! COME ON! You know what?! Demons!!" They have been summoned. "Oh good, you're in good health. Go to earth quickly, and both those guardians have the lying sin.

GO!" They nodded and vanished. On Earth, both Sashell and Britannia were flying with the lying sin in Sashell's hand. "What are we supposed to do?"

"Let's go back to the house, maybe Ida will do something with this." Says Britannia. "An attack came, and the girls crashed down, and Sashell let go of the sin.

"No." She looked up and it was the previous demons they were fighting. They were coming down. Britannia quickly got up and grabbed the sin. "Sashell!"

"No, Go! I'll take care of them," says Sashell.

"All by yourself?" "We don't have time. Get to the house or summoned Ida, I don't know. VENUS BEAM!" A huge beam blasted towards them, but they dodged. "Ugh, they have gotten stronger. Time to use, Sun aura." Then both Sashell and Britannia vanished.

"What? Where did they go?" Asked Chloe.

"I don't know." "I know where they went." says the Anti-Christ walking up. "My lord, where could have they gone?" Asked Glenn.

"They have been teleported by Dave...Zeus." They all gasped. To where?"

"Antarctica. I feel their presence there; I'm going to give you some of my powers and use some of Fire's powers to get that lying sin. You'll be fast enough to get it and get back to hell." They all nodded. The Marry Warriors have been summoned to Sapphire's kitchen.

"What the-We didn't teleport here? Who summoned us?" Asked Julmarie. "I did." They turned around following that voice and noticed an incredible aura towards this person.

"W-Who are you? This aura...?" "Wait, you must be Zeus?" Asked Monica.

"Yes." "How did you-?" Asked Ally.

"I don't know; it's like I guess." "That's one of my abilities. I am a God. The messiah as well. My name is Zeus, but I like to be called Dave. I am the second child of God after Jesus Christ. I'm here to tell you what to do. You're going to make the Holy Grail to heal your friends, and don't worry about Sapphire. She's chatting with her other triplet sister Starfire, alongside with

Roderick. Also, with the lying sin. Sashell and Britannia have it and they're in Antarctica."

Twenty-Six

FINAL BATTLE PART II

Sapphire woke up in a white baby green, blue room. There she saw Roderick.

"Roderick? Where am I? What is this?" She crawls towards him and shakes him. "Roderick? Roderick?" He was woken up. Huh? Where am I? How did I fall asleep?? Sapphire?"

"I don't know what's going on either, but I think someone is waiting for us."

"It's me." they turned around and looked and was in shock. "Hello.

I am Starfire; you're another sister. We're triplets," says a ghost girl. "Wait, you're a ghost..." "Not really. I am a spiritual ghost. I possessed one of the trinities, The Holy Spirit." "Oh. Wait how did I fall asleep. God warriors or any warriors don't need no sleep." 'I put you asleep when you were watching her. We're going to heal her after the rage she was in. A God warrior can do just as much of a messiah can do. Roderick, fuse with me?"

"Wait, we can do fusion?"

"Yes, many warriors, even angels back in heaven, can do fusion. But only with their kind. The only way you can do fusion with others who are not even your kind if you're a true God."

"Wait, not even the trinities can help?" Asked Sapphire.

"Nope. You got to be over omi-ponent."

"Oh." "How to fuse." "Well, I don't blame you for not remembering. We first got to glow. Like this." She started to glow yellow. "Try." He closed his eyes and tried. "I can't do this."

"Well, you better hurry. The Marry Warriors are making a holy grail to heal Sapphire human form; we need to heal her warrior form." "Wait, I'm not fully healed?"

"Nope, Sapphire, that you did was so powerful it can destroy the whole omniverse and every verse inside of it. You could've easily destroyed even infinity, but due to the fact that you been reborn, it took longer. Also, the Lying Sin was found."

"It was what?" 'Who was it?"

"Your aunt Neata, and right now, she's dying.

There are demons who are different, and a lot stronger who you faced before, and the other warriors are fighting them. The Anti-Christ was soon to be here, but Dave arrived, and he got shot down. The God Warriors were going to injure him more, but he escaped and Sashell and Britannia been teleported to Antarctica, and the demons will soon be there. The two have the lying sin with them, so we must hurry." The two were in shock.

"Okay, I'll try." "You know what? Forget it. You know how to heal?" "Yes." "Since when?" Asked Sapphire, surprised.

"I learn from you, Sapphire." He raised his hand out and gray aura appeared. The two started to heal Sapphire. Downstairs, The Marry warriors were talking to Dave.

"Why transfer them there? To the coldest content?" "So, Sapphire be there, and they're going to meet other guardians like them. Also, you got to help the warriors. The Anti-Christ escape them, and he gave some of his powers to the previous demons you battled, to travel to Antarctica, and besides, you need to make this Holy Grail cause only Marry warriors know how to make it, it'll heal the warriors and Sapphire ever since her rage form, just pour it in her and she'll be good as new, she's still a little injured from what happened."

"Oh, I see, and that's it?" "Yes, hurry up and make it. Here's the holy golden cup." He summoned it. "How do we make it?"

"You'll know. Sapphire needs this to travel to that continent and get rid of that sin once and for all.

"Can't you do it." "Not a part of this show. Only she can. The demons used her power to search for the lying sin, and it was inside of the Jesus Warriors mother."

"[GASPED]. Neata?" Asked Josh. "Yes. Now make the Holy grail to get rid of those demons once and for all." They nodded. He disappeared. "It looks like the reason Sapphire can destroy it cause of the sun's heat," says Julmarie.

"That is true, also how do we know what to do? To make this Holy Grail?" Asked Re-Re.

"Hey, let's use our Marry warrior aura towards the cup," says Winston.

"Oh, right." They all started to glow in their dwarf planets colors, and they reached their hands out to the cup. It transferred to the cup and it made white milk inside, and it started to change color.

"We did it." Shouted Selena. "We're black, black people don't say that," says Sheldon. "Geez racism." Says Cory. "It's kind of true," says Xavier. "Doesn't matter, let's just get this to Sapphire so she can transfer to Antarctica and help her sisters," says Josh.

Over at the cold continent, Sashell and Britannia got up and was in huge shocked to see where they are. 'Ah! It's cold. Where are we?" Asked Britannia.

"Judging by this, it thinks either the North pole or Antarctica," says Sashell. Then a blast was coming towards them, but then, Britannia used a shield to block it. What the-? Who was that? I can't see them." Then Another came and it hit Sashell and she got hit.

"Ah!" The sin fell, and it was being covered by snow, but then a demon picked it up. 'We got what we came for. "I can't see them! Ugh!" She attacked everywhere, but no one got hit. "They're invisible. They got the sin!"

Then an attack came, and it hit one of the demons who had the sin. The sin was slipping away, and Sashell went and grabbed it. "Who was that? You?" "No." Sashell flew towards the sin, but then Chloe attacked her, and she got hit. "Ugh, I could've sworn I dodged that." Then another attack was appearing behind her, but Britannia used one of her attacks and countered it. Britannia was running towards the sin, but Chloe grabbed it, but then a halo attack came, and it hit Chloe and the sin was flying towards the sky. Sashell then grabbed it and landed.

"I can't see." Then the mist appeared. "Huh?" She then sees invisible bodies around and one was coming towards her and it hit her. It then grabbed the sin, but then Britannia attack him and he fell. Sashell kicked the body and grabbed the sin.

"Let's get out of here, but then, the bodies appeared right in front of them and started to form. "What are they? Actually, where this mist comes from?" Asked Sashell.

They fused into one giant demon. "What the hell?" The demon begins to attack them, and they dodged. It swishes out of the mist.

"Oh, no!" Britannia started to blast it even dough the mist was gone; she remembers where it was. But the attack was going through.

"What the-How?" Then Britannia got punched down. Sashell quickly sees an attack where Britannia got hit, but there was no smoke.

"What is going on?" She then was felt like she was getting squeezed.

"AH!!" "Sashell." It grabbed the lying sin and threw Sashell away.

"SASHELL!!" Yelled her little sister, but then Britannia saw a shadow, and it was ready to stomp on her, but then an attack came, and it hit them. It was a blue beam.

"Huh? Then seven people came and attacked the creature. One came holding Sashell. "Sashell..." Says Britannia in shocked and relieved that her sister is okay. One person used mist to see the see-through body. 'What other guardians?! UGH!" Yelled the monster as he attacked. Back at the house, the Marry Warriors were still in the kitchen ready to deliver the grail to Sapphire.

"Alright, the grail is ready, so we can now deliver it to her," says Re-Re.

"Wait! Let's take a sample," says Serena.

"Why?" Asked Winston.

"I don't know. Maybe because I want some." She replies back with her tongue out like she wants some.

"Alright, let's get some." Says Selena. They took some cups out of the cabinet. They took a sample. "Wow! The is delicious, "says Elizabeth. Then they started to glow of their planet's colors.

"Huh? What's going on?" Asked Xavier. Then their Angel Fairy appeared out, but they were still transformed. "What the-Oh my," says Fairy of Ce-Ce.

"What's going on? How come we still transforms... without you...?"

"That's because of the Holy Grail. You can now transform without us."

"Holy...We need to send this to everybody." "But sometimes I like having the Angel fairies around," says Sheldon. "That's nice, but it's time for us to head back to Heaven," says Angel fairy of Pluto.

"Wait, but you're named after our planets. Shouldn't you be able to get back there?" Asked Josh.

"Oh, goodness, no. Those planets are dense, even in the omniverse, the omniverse still couldn't heal them because of their moons. It's up to you guys to save them, and maybe the people in it..."

"Wait, there are people living there too? So, the planets must've been like earth, then." "Eh...Kind of." "Just give the Holy grail to Sapphire, not all of it and gave it to your friends, but probably give most to Roderick." "Why most to him?" Asked Winston.

"God warriors are rare. Like very rare. If you give him mostly, it can transfer to the other five remaining God warriors who are on the battlefield. But save the rest for the others. Maybe after the battle."

"Okay." They ran upstairs and entered her room. "Man, they're both asleep." Says Julmarie.

"Or just meeting Starfire," says Re-Re. Inside the dream, "Roderick, you're soon going to wake up."

"What?" "Yeah, the God warriors are going to put the Holy Grail in you, and you're going to wake up.... maybe just about now." He vanished, and he was woken up.

"Huh? Where...Marry warriors...?" Then he started to glow white. "What is this?" He asked, looking at himself. His angel fairy appeared.

"The holy grail. You now can transform without me." Says his angel fairy. "Seriously...?" "Yes, and now thanks to you, the other God warriors on the battlefield are the same as you."

"Wow. Guys I met-" "We know. Starfire." "How did you-" "We met Starfiria brother. Zeus."

"Wait...What?" "Yeah. No time to explain. The other warriors need us. Let's give her the holy grail," says Julmarie. "Will you two just hook up already?" He started to blush. "We're just friends, that's all."

"Enough already. Let's give her the grail and help the others." Says Xavier. In her dream, Starfire stops healing.

"Well, that's it, your angel form is now complete, and now they're going to Holy Grail, also need I remind you; you can now transform without your angel fairy."

"What? How? Is the Holy Grail really that special?"

"Yes. The Holy grail was made by Marry, and her warriors made it. It's so powerful you can now transform without your fairy. We probably have no time. You'll see me again."

"Starfire...Thank you." She nodded her head, and Sapphire was awoken. Huh? What's going on?" She asked raising up?"

"You were sleeping, but now not to explain. We need to hurry up." "Yes, but I need to go to Antarctica. I feel something. I feel new energy. Like more planet powers, and it's at Antarctica." "Why there?" Asked Josh.

"Maybe because they been teleported there?" Asked Elizabeth. "Maybe. Let's go, Sapphire." She started to glow white and she had a white gown only and been teleported. "W-Where has she gone?" "Maybe where the guardians are. Let's go. We'll leave this here," says Julmarie. On the battlefield.

The Jesus warriors were still using their elements to blow the new demons away with the help of the God warriors. "I can't believe this; we can now teleport without our fairies. I wonder how." Asked Meisha.

"We'll ask about that later, right now, Focus!" Shouted Junior. The Marry warriors appeared and used attacks on the demons.

"Alright now shits about to get real! HA!!" A huge white explosion appeared. The marry warriors flew down and grabbed the Jesus and Marry warriors before they got hit, and the demons got killed.

"Holy. Roderick...You did that?" Asked Allyson.

"Who else?"

"Where did you get that power?" Asked Junior.

"The Holy Grail. There's not enough; I poured most of it in me so it can be connected to you. See how you can see your fairy while still being transform and, Oh, my God, what happens to aunty Neata?" Asked Roderick flying to her.

"It turned out she has the lying sin."

"Oh, wait to hold on, how come you guys aren't transforming without - oh forget it, this season is basically off you guys." Says Roderick. "Yeah, and where's Sapphire?" asked Abigail, flying up.

"Antarctica. She's gonna blew it up with the rest of the guardians. There new ones." Says Roderick.
"Wait, new guardians?"

"Yeah. We should probably- ah who cares, they're gonna blow it up. It's how the creator wrote it," says Tristan.

"Geez, so much fourth wall breaks," says Allyson. At Antarctica, the guardians were still fighting the demon.
"Ugh, will you guys just hold-" Then Sashell came across the sin and split it. "Damn it!" They both said.

"I only cut half." Says Sashell landing with it. "It vanished. "Where does it go?" Asked Britannia.

"Look!" Says Saturn. The sin was disappearing. "Sashell, you son of a- That's it everyone dies!" It had a huge red energy and expanded it through, and the Guardians were badly injured. Then Sapphire appeared and cut off his arm. "Sapphire...?" says Sashell, injured. 'I have no time here; the sin is vanishing. If it's in hell, it'll stop vanishing, but as I was fighting, I set a bomb with the power of the anti-Christ power into this land, so strong it'll wipe the planet.' He thought with his mind.

"Get ready, you guys; we're going to blow this continent up." "What? Why?" Asked Neptune. "You must be the new guardians, I sense you, and also, I just read his mind. He has the Anti-Christ power. Sashell and Britannia, you have a tiny bit of Zeus power in you. He teleports you here with a tiny bit of his power, that's why you're still alive against this monster, the same goes for your new ones, am I correct?"

"You're right about the teleport one, wait, you can now read people's minds?" Asked Jupiter.

"Yup, just how I learn reality-bending." "Then why now-" "Because it's the point of the show, and so it can have longer seasons. Oh my God..."

"I'll kill you!!!" Yelled the monster as it throws a huge beam. "He never throws that kind of beam before we got here." Says Sashell.

"No need." Sapphire used protection.

"Guys call. Hold on to me." They were all holding on to each other than lead to both Sashell and Britannia towards Sapphire. "Call out your planet power and transfer it to me, and we'll blow up this continent." They nodded. "Jupiter power!" "Saturn Power!" "Uranus Power!" "Neptune power!"

"Keplter power!" "Venus power!" They all glowed aura, and they fused with Sapphire into an orange glow person. The force-field shine brighter and larger ad it hit the demons, but they vanished. Antarctica started to glow red and starting to blow up. The fusion summoned a staff and threw it the land. E.J. teleported to the core and fused with it.

"EARTH!!!" He was controlling the earth so that it won't explode. Antarctica blew up. The fusion teleported to the moon as the land been explode, but not the earth. They un-fused. Sapphire was back to her normal transformation. "That form...It didn't last much.

Aww." "Hey, you guys...now that you're here," says Sashell. "We won't be joining you."

"Says what...?" Asked Sapphire. "I'm sorry, we were just here to destroy the lying sin, but half of it is gone. Now we have to wait-

"You're one of us. Fight with us." Says Britannia. "We're sorry." Jupiter summoned a portal, and they been sucked into it and reunited with everyone.

"Whoa. Guys, are you okay?" Asked Abigail. "Yeah, we just met new warriors who just like us..." "Other planets." "Then where are they?" "They don't want to be with us." "I don't understand. Why?" "They never gave us a real reason, and they just only said they're here for the lying sin."

"How did they get their powers? Angel fairies?" 'Nope, I don't sense other angel fairies around," says Angel fairy of earth teleporting with Sonny.

"Then they must be the first one before us who can't transform without our fairies," says Josh. "How? They don't have the Holy Grail," says Julmarie.

"Maybe they met Marry," says Selena.

"Revival," says sonny towards his mother. She was back to normal. "Wait, it was inside her?"

"Of course. Now she's alive. God warriors, if you don't mind?" "No need. I wish everything were back to normal and Neata forget what happened this night," says Sapphire. Everything was back to normal.

"Finally, it's over..." "Not really..." says Sashell.

"What do you mean?" Asked Shquana.

"I was so dumb, I only destroyed half the lying sin, and they got away, it looks like they been summoned when we did a blast towards them as a fusion.

"You guys, fused? Wait, can we fuse?" Asked Rihanna.

"Yeah, Starfire explained it to me when I met her. I was originally supposed to fuse with her." Says Roderick, "Starfire? You mean Starfiria?" Asked Tristan.

"Nope, Starfire. Sapphire other triplet sisters." "Wait, so you have another sister? How are you a triplet?" Asked Gabriella. "

I don't know. Now well, everything is back to normal." says Sapphire. "We also need to see who those guardians are." "We'll see them soon. Do you guys want the Holy Grail?" Asked Julmarie. They nodded and was at Sapphire's room.

"Alright, here's the holy grail," says the fairies. God warriors used psychic powers and controlled the liquid.

"Since when the-" "We just now learning it." They hand it to the Jesus warriors and the two guardians, as they open their mouth, the warriors drink it.

"Hmm... So delicious. Marry is such a good cooker," says Britannia. Then their angel fairies came out. "Hmm, we're finally out," says Angel fairy of Mercury. "Now, we can go to heaven." Says Angel of Venus. "Really? You're not going to stay, even with Guinea?"

"Normally, I would've gone back to the Zettaverse, but Jesus told me to stay for the future events," says Guinea transforming to his human form. "Wait, you had a human-Okay; can we just end this episode already?"

"Damn so quickly?" "Yeah. I need to go home and sleep or some shit. Have fun in heaven, Angel fairies. We hope to see you again," says Roman. They all nodded and vanished.

"Now we'll see what's Satan plotting. See you all in Season 2, Chapter 27. Last 4th wall break. Later."